Memsahib

Attention Authors

Manas Publications is fighting a war to tell the world that India can win the battle not only by the bullet but also by the pen. We are converting fighters into writers. There is no dearth of intellectuals in our country, however, their knowledge is confined to them only. No sincere effort has been made by any other publisher to give the right direction to their knowledge and the talent of every intellectual is lying hidden. An author always presents the raw material in the shape of a manuscript and it is the job of the publisher to convert it to a finished product. Manas has been continually motivating intellectuals and publishing their manuscripts for more than two decades and would like to publish your manuscript too. If you or your colleagues have a manuscript ready for publication or are working on it, contact us with a detailed synopsis and list of contents. Manas will also suggest you a suitable title for writing related to your area of expertise. Manas is known for its publishing quality. We take utmost care in publishing and also give wide publicity to the book and its author through our national and international distribution network.

Memsahib

A Novel by

Aparna Jha

Manas Publications
New Delhi-110002 (INDIA)

Manas Publications
(Publishers, Distributors, Importers & Exporters)
4402/5A, Main Ansari Road,
(Opp. HDFC Bank), Darya Ganj,
New Delhi - 110 002 (INDIA)
Ph.: 23260783, 23265523:, 23842660 (R)
Fax: 011-23272766
E-mail: manaspublications@vsnl.com
www.manaspublications.in

2009

ISBN 978-81-7049-351-8
Rs. 295

Typeset at
Manas Publications

Printed in India at
Jaico Printers, Delhi
and Published by Mrs Suman Lata for
Manas Publications, 4402/5A, Main Ansari Road,
Opp. HDFC Bank, Darya Ganj,
New Delhi - 110 002 (INDIA)

Contents

Preface

My first book, a collection of short stories, was published in 2004. It took me five years to publish the second one.

Lives of men and women have undergone a sea change in the past fifteen to twenty years, especially in metros. Relationships are getting re-defined. Women are freer and do not hesitate to experiment, to seek new-found pleasures. And the society seems to be more tolerant towards things that would have been frowned upon a generation back.

If a man can seek pleasure, so can a woman. Simran is smart, erudite. Yet, her husband Varun cheats her.

Simran leaves Delhi and shifts to Chennai. She goes to the beach, looks at the waves, very beautiful. Like the sea which is answerable to none, she feels she is a free woman.

She hits back and gets involved with a younger man.

Varun has an affair with Swati, his junior. Yet, he refuses to commit. Swati moves on. She marries another man.

Man is no longer in complete control.

The *'Memsahib'* seeks to explore fragile human relationships. Simran, mother of a grown up son, goes to William. She feels desired; but this leaves her more dissatisfied. William is no angel.

Perfect happiness is mirage-like. Commitments are no longer sacred. Pleasure is the keyword.

This book is an attempt to delve into human psyche in the contemporary world without being judgmental.

Aparna Jha

1

GOA

The waves howled like a bunch of women in labour; part alluring, part scary. They wailed, in intense pain, not knowing whether they would survive to see the morrow. The palm trees stooped to comfort, as a gust of wind blew.

Suddenly they all laughed. Loudly. They had realized the futility of it. How could death be so scary when none of them knew what it looked like.

Within an hour, they were all soothed.

The sun shone brightly.

A new day had been born.

A few years ago Simran and Varun were in Goa. The beautiful, golden beaches with small, toy like homes under trees, a different world. The Portuguese had left an indelible mark on the land and its people.

They had checked into a tourist resort in Panjim, by the side of river Mandavi. They took a ferry in the evening, sipped feni, the local brew, and watched Portuguese and Konkani dances.

Varun got up, held Simran's hands, and took her to the spot where the dancers swayed and swerved, the way he would direct her when they made love.

They came back, exhausted, spread on the narrow bed and slept, their bags lying unpacked.

Next morning Simran woke up early. She went to the bathroom. The hissing sea was furious; she could hear. She stood there for a while, as it groaned, beckoning her.

She opened the door and ran hurriedly towards her husband.

'Let's go to Calangute today,' she whispered into his ears. It was hot and he had spread out both his legs, like blades of scissors.

'Ummm….,' he replied.

She had worn a red swimsuit with a flower painted at the centre.

She entered the sea, felt the waves surge forward, and then recede. As she stood there, she loved the sea frothing at her feet. They played with water for an hour or two. Then they spread their towels on the sand.

It was hot. The clothes stuck to their bodies like band-aid. They had coconut water. The vendor sliced off the top of a coconut with his sharp edged blade, and inserted a pipe into it. He handed it over to Varun.

Simran looked at miles and miles of water. She laughed. Varun looked at her, puzzled. 'Man always remains in awe of Nature,' she said, 'Nature has to show its fury only once and all his pride is washed away.'

Simran thought of her dead sister. Simran always bowed her head before the lofty mountains, and the mighty sea.

She had seen their anger.

Varun clicked Simran, black sky in the background, her feet digging into golden sand. Her nails, painted red, were buried in sand, as her hair flew on her face. She was wearing small, golden earrings; two semicircles, with intricate patterns. Her legs were bare. Varun said she looked great in that photograph.

They came back to their room, late at night. Varun switched on the TV. As Simran undressed, Varun held her from behind. She shivered as his fingers crawled on her face, her small and round breasts, her flat belly. He touched her belly button and kissed it lightly. The sea roared outside as she sat on a high-backed chair, on Varun's lap. He held her, exploring her, tasting her, savouring her. His moustaches, slightly bushy, tickled her as he bent to kiss her.

Simran started playing with the hair on his chest, peeping through his shirt, unbuttoned. Varun lighted a cigarette. The room was filled with music and the smell of tobacco.

They woke up late the next morning and went for a conducted tour to South Goa, with churches and temples.

They also went to Dauna Paula, the place lovers never miss. The white statues of the two lovers stood on the seashore, at some height. They climbed on to the spot, Simran slipping at times.

The sea was enchanting. They leaned against the iron railings, painted white, with leafless trees behind them. Varun placed his hand on Simran's shoulder, as she stood.

Simran smiled, as a passerby turned back and gave them an indulgent look.

They spent the last two days in a small cottage on Miramar Beach.

2

THE SON

They returned to Delhi soon afterward. Simran taught political science and Varun was a lawyer.

After a few years of struggle, they led comfortable lives. They had a son, in ten plus two. Bunny, their son, resembled his mother in many ways. He had taken her complexion, and had common sense. He was ambitious, always dreamt of making it big.

His friends would come to his place often, during evenings. They would smoke, and discuss chicks. At times they watched a match on television.

Since the past few months, Simran had become irritable. She hardly saw Varun.

He was not bothered. Varun was busy with his junior. Simran suspected he was thick with her. Simran and Varun had been married for a long time. Simran felt jealous when she saw Varun with his junior, Swati. She felt her husband needed her no longer.

Simran was tall, slightly bulky. Her lips were wafer-thin; and they had a way of spreading out and making a semi-circle when she smiled. Though not strikingly beautiful, she was considered good looking by many.

Varun hardly showed any interest in family matters. He only thought of Swati. He thought of new ways to please her, love her.

Simran tried not to think about them. Her thoughts shifted towards her son.

She often saw Bunny leave the house without informing anyone. Simran would panic. He would be back in an hour, his hands loaded with books. Simran tried searching for anything else he had brought. She usually found nothing.

Simran felt restless. She went to the balcony. She loved sitting there, early in the morning. A small bird, grey and black in colour, with a thin, narrow neck, sat on the railing, and chirped. Simran watched it intently. It jumped from one end to the other, making noise. It sat on the rubber plant, at its tip, and opened its mouth and then shut it. This went on for sometime. It was joined by another bird.

She came back to her room. Soon their maidservant, Sunita, brought her a glass of milk. She placed it carefully on her study table.

'You look quite lost nowadays,' she asked with her eyes fixed on the floor.

'Bunny baba also behaves strangely,' she continued.

Simran finally shut the book in her hands.

'What have you seen?'

'Nothing.' The maid looked at her mistress calmly.

She had come to this family when she was a child, and she was concerned now.

'What have you seen Bunny do?' Simran chewed every word she spoke.

'I have seen him sit with his friends and snort some powder.' This time Sunita looked at her directly.

Simran went to the washroom. She washed her face, applied night cream, and went to bed.

She could not sleep.

3

The Junior

Varun spent more time with Swati. Both of them prepared the cases together. Swati was hardworking, she helped Varun in his work. Drafting, filing, arguing–she did these jobs single-handedly. She had no hassles about going to the registry, running from one table to the other, getting cases filed. Varun charged a hefty fee for drafting and filing cases.

When the others left the office, they found some excuse to stay back. Swati would often ring up her mother.

'Ma, I have to argue a case tomorrow. I have to do some research.'

'Will you be late?'

'Yes, Ma. Ask Papa to eat.'

Her mother waited for her.

At times she asked, 'Why don't you do research at home?'

'I don't have the books, or the Case Finder.'

Her mother was not convinced.

'Are you the only junior Varun has?'

'No. There are others,' she evaded. 'But I am trusted.'

'I have to work hard to rise in my profession.' She ate as she spoke.

Swati's mother gave her a penetrating look. 'Your sisters are married and your father is always worried about you.'

Swati washed her hands quickly and went to her room. She tried marking out the relevant portions of the matter she had to argue. She could not concentrate. Her mind was elsewhere. Her association with Varun had changed her life. Life without him seemed meaningless. She did not think of the future. She was not bothered. She was happy the way things were.

On Sundays, Swati did not go to the office. She helped her mother in the kitchen, talked to her father.

'A lawyer should be benevolent,' her father advised, 'and treat poor clients kindly.'

'But you should do justice to all your cases,' he continued, smiling at his daughter, 'and should not be bothered about the result.'

Her mother listened carefully to such discussions. She did not speak much.

'I think women should teach, if at all they want to work for a living.'

She did not like her daughter keeping late hours.

'When you are married, and have children, it will be difficult for you to cope.'

Her father would be irritated. 'Can't you think beyond marriage and children?'

'A woman has certain responsibilities. A teacher's job is not taxing.'

'My daughter has talent,' Swati had a fond father, 'she will earn a name for herself.'

Swati was cheerful when the weekend was over. She looked forward to meeting Varun. She went to the court, wore her coat and gown, and attended to the cases.

During evening, after their cases had been heard, they drove back to Varun's office. Swati loved the drive. She talked non-stop, as Varun listened.

'How old are you?' Varun asked. Swati was fresh out of the law college, she had to be in her early twenties. Varun explained things to her strenuously. He worked hard with her, taught her how to handle cases.

Swati looked smart, and had the right contours. Youth was on her side. Just as a child loves showing off a new toy, Swati loved displaying her body. She looked studious, but was attractive. Her face had a freshness which many found alluring.

After seven in the evening, when others had left, they did no work. They sat chatting, talking of nothing in particular. Swati asked Varun about his family, friends. She talked about her childhood, her sisters. Varun usually sat close to her, almost touching her.

Once Swati went to the washroom, Varun followed her. He pressed his body against hers. Her body was reflected in the mirror. He held her, pressed her again and again. They came back to his chamber, discussed cases. Then they left.

Others in the office knew something was brewing between them. They saw it in their eyes.

Varun was careful. But Swati was not bothered. She loved Varun, and did not care about what the others said.

While returning home, Swati was quiet. She thought about Varun and the time spent with him.

One day Swati met Varun's wife in a Shopping Mall. She looked for a watch, while Simran wanted to buy a nose stud.

'My wife,' Varun introduced.

Simran nodded.

'Nice meeting you,' saying so, she clicked her heels and went away.

Swati stared at her.

She walked aimlessly in the Mall for the next few hours. She hopped from one shop to the other, looking at knickknacks, jewellery, clothes. A small vase, kept in the glass case, caught her fancy.

'What is its price?' she enquired.

The shopkeeper was busy. He was attending to another customer.

She decided to come back later. Simran had looked striking in green chiffon. Swati wanted to talk to her.

Simran did not like her. Swati knew. Simran's eyes bore a hostile expression. Whenever she received her calls on Varun's mobile, she disconnected.

Varun hardly talked to Swati in Simran's presence.

Swati came back to the shop.

'Rupees eighteen hundred and fifty,' the shopkeeper quoted the price.

'No discount?'

'Sorry. It is a fixed price shop.'

Having made the payment, she left the shop. The shops looked like boxes, all in a row.

She went up the escalator, and bought candy floss. It stuck to her mouth like sticky cotton. She unzipped her purse, took a handkerchief, and wiped it off.

Varun sent an SMS to her. He was in the lobby. Simran had gone. He offered to show her a movie in the multiplex.

'No,' Swati declined. 'Some other day.'

4

Cocaine

Sunita caught Bunny snorting cocaine. She dragged him to his parents' bedroom. 'Leave me,' the boy tried disentangling himself. Sunita tightened her grip.

Simran sprang to her feet.

'What is this?'

'It is my friend's.'

'No,' Sunita intervened, 'I saw him take it.'

Varun dragged him by his hair. 'Get out,' he shouted, shutting the door behind him.

Bunny shivered outside. He had never seen his father in such anger.

'This boy has been cheating us,' Varun was fuming. 'No one will let him in.'

Bunny looked around. He hoped none of his neighbours saw him.

It was late at night.

Simran was equally harsh. She shut all the windows of her room.

It was cold. Bunny wore a sleeveless pullover. The neighbourhood was quiet. After more than two hours, Sunita opened the door.

Bunny was sitting near the gate, his hands covering his face.

Sunita touched his sleeves. He looked up.

'Sahib has gone off to sleep,' she spoke gently. 'Eat something.'

She had brought vegetables and *poori* on a small plate. Bunny ate hungrily. He had a glass of water. Sunita sat beside him.

'When sahib went off to sleep, memsahib got up stealthily, and asked me to get you some food.'

Bunny looked at the moon, a big yellow ball. He had never seen his father in such anger.

Simran was in her room. She cried.

'Did he eat?'

'Yes.'

'Now go to sleep.' There was determination in her eyes. 'Let him stay out the whole night.'

When Sunita opened the door the next morning, she saw Bunny. He was curled up, sleeping near the gate.

Varun got up, and went to his son. He brought him inside.

Varun touched his son lightly. He loved him.

Bunny was no longer allowed to go out alone. Sunita accompanied him to his school. She sat near the playground, as Bunny attended his classes. Bunny felt embarrassed. He did not want his friends to know Sunita came with him everyday.

By afternoon, Simran was back from her college. She took him for his tuition.

His friends were not allowed inside the house. They handed over books to Sunita, at the gate.

Sunita slept in Bunny's room, on the floor.

At times Bunny was restless. The women would sit with him, talk to him.

'Concentrate on your studies. Everything will be alright.'

Varun had taken back Bunny's mobile phone. Sunita brought him tea every two hours.

'When you are a doctor,' she said, sitting near him, 'I will be your first patient.'

Bunny looked at her vaguely. He had seen his friend die.

He studied hard. He was regaining interest in his books. His mother sat with him, helping him. Sunita brought him tea, coffee, food.

Varun went straight to his son's room when he came back from the office. He sat with his laptop, drafting the matters, as Bunny studied in a corner. Simran lay on her bed, waiting for Varun. Her husband usually came very late. He yawned, and went off to sleep within minutes. Then he would dream of his junior.

Simran looked at the ceiling for a long time. She slept much after Varun did.

Varun took Bunny for his premedical tests.

Since Bunny had eaten nothing before he went to take his examination, Varun took him to a restaurant immediately after the examination was over.

Once Swati saw him, as he was entering a restaurant. Bunny's examinations were almost over. It was around two in the afternoon, the sun blazed. Swati took out the sun glasses and looked at Varun, with some surprise.

Bunny looked tired.

Swati pulled a chair for him. They sipped coke. After about five minutes, Swati left.

'Your son is handsome.' Swati told Varun afterwards.

Varun sounded worried. 'I hope he clears his entrance test.'

'How is he keeping otherwise?'

'We don't leave him alone for a minute. We have seized his mobile. We don't let his friends enter the house.'

Swati looked sympathetically. She carried a purse, with small flowers embroidered.

'Nice purse. Where did you buy it from?'

'From a local market. It is two minutes walk from my home.'

'I want a similar one for my wife.'

Swati did not respond.

'You take care of all the cases tomorrow. I have to go with my son.'

Swati looked at the list. Many cases were listed. She wondered how she would manage.

'I will come back as soon as possible.'

Varun sensed Swati looked worried.

'Tomorrow is my son's last test.'

Swati smiled. 'No problem. I will manage.'

That is what he liked about Swati. She could manage things. He could not trust any other junior with his cases.

The result was declared. Bunny had cleared the CPMT entrance test. He had also done well in his ten plus two examinations.

They went to a temple in the evening. Simran thanked God, fervently hoping her son would not resume taking drugs.

Simran's brother came at night.

'Well done,' he patted Bunny on his back.

They had dinner together. Bunny spoke a lot. He felt good.

Bunny trained to become a doctor.

5

Varun Made No Promises

They did not venture out, remained indoor. Hot wind blew, as the birds shouted, breaking the silence. The trees stood erect, with flaming orange and yellow flowers. Tender saplings wilted, like the drooping under lip.

Varun rested his head against his chair.

Swati stood behind him. She massaged his head gently, in slow motion.

Varun felt relaxed. He shut his eyes, as Swati's fingers crawled on his forehead. He felt strangely at peace. He pulled Swati on his lap, and licked her ears.

Swati shut her eyes.

'Why did you refuse to watch the movie with me?'

'Ma had given me a deadline.'

'Let us go today.' Varun looked at her with anticipation.

By the time they reached the theatre, the movie had begun. They had missed the first five minutes.

They hardly watched the movie. Varun touched Swati, again and again. He removed her slippers, caressed her feet.

The movie was soon over. A woman in a black spaghetti top walked ahead of them.

Swati stared at her. Suddenly the woman looked back and smiled. Swati could recognize her faintly. Where had they met?

The woman walked up to her. 'I am Nafisa. We were together in the school.'

'Oh,' now she recognized. They had studied in the same class, but in different sections.

Swati did not introduce Varun to her. Nafisa threw an inquisitive look at him. She said goodbye and left. Swati heaved a sigh of relief.

Nafisa had asked her later, when they met again, in a coffee shop. 'Who was that man with you?'

'My senior.'

'Oh, I see.'

Swati tried changing the topic.

'Are you working?'

'I work with a television channel.'

It was a crowded place. They had coffee together.

'Are you married?'

'I have a live-in relationship.'

Swati looked at her.

'My partner works with the same television channel.'

'What about you?'

Swati evaded looking at her. There was pressure on her to marry. 'I am single. If my mother had her way, I would have been married, with four children by now.'

Nafisa laughed. 'These mothers!'

'I keep odd timings,' Swati added, 'I cannot afford to marry right now.'

'I want to rise in my field,' Swati continued, as Nafisa looked at her smilingly. 'I need at least two years before I settle down.'

'I need five.'

'Live-in relationship is most convenient. Both the parties can maintain their independence,' she added.

Swati nodded.

Suddenly she started perspiring. Drops of sweat erupted, swathing her, running down her forehead. She wiped her face with a handkerchief.

Varun was married, and he loved his son.

6

Turbulence

A party was thrown when Bunny was to go to his medical college for his professional course. He stood at the entrance, greeting the guests, ushering them in. They sat in the lawn, their chairs pulled closer, as soft music played in the background. Ms Singh, Simran's colleague, asked Bunny to come to her. She patted him and gave him a lecture on the advantages of eating green vegetables, fruits, and drinking milk, more so when one is in a hostel. Her granddaughter, Cookie, sipped Coke.

Bunny had a close group of friends. Bunny had many girls coming to him as he was good in studies, and he did not mind sharing his notes with them. Raj had got through IIT, Kharagpur, Supreeta was aiming to train at Bangalore Law School, and Ranjit was joining the IMA at Dehradun. They had their future before them.

Lunch was served. They wound up soon. Bunny had to leave the following day and they had a lot of packing to do.

Varun and Bunny drove down to his college early in the morning. The place was about hundred kilometres from Delhi, largely uninhabited.

They could see a huge, red building. Lush lawns could be seen on both sides, covered with bright flowers. White candy tufts made a semicircular wreath at the centre; with a sprinkling of roses elsewhere. They went up a flight of steps, huge flower pots on both the sides. The Principal's room was at the end of the corridor.

It was quite late at night when Varun returned. Simran was sitting on her bed, her head propped against the pillow, as she prepared for her classes the next day.

'Mr. Chandwani rang up,' Simran informed, as Varun entered his bedroom. Mr. Chandwani was Varun's associate.

'Listen,' Mr. Chandwani spoke when Varun rang him up, 'I am flying to London in a week. You may have to come along.'

Simran was alone. The son was in the hostel, the husband on tour. She drove to her college, took her classes and came back. Life was simple, and boring. She yearned to hear her mobile ring. At times she called up both, one after the other. They were busy, they couldn't talk to her. Simran felt she was a superfluous baggage in their life.

They had gone to Mahabaleshwar sometime back, during summer. It rained heavily, and it was pure bliss to walk on misty roads, with trees and bushes on both sides. Drenched in water, they walked, and drank strawberry shake. Looking back wistfully, she yearned to re-live those days. Now her husband hardly had any time for her. She had a vague feeling her husband had taken Swati, his junior, along with him to London.

Once she had seen a notepad in her husband's suitcase. It had childish scribbling. Simran had a suspicion that Swati travelled with her husband on tours. Studious, and with thick glasses, Swati was attractive in her own way.

It was raining. A spark of lightning shot like an arrow, as it thundered. Simran shut all the windows. She sat alone in her bedroom, as raindrops fell noisily. She felt sad, she had never felt so lonely and purposeless. She had heard women commit suicide out of sheer boredom.

She called up her mother. 'Hello,' her father shouted, unable to hear her clearly. She told him that she would be coming over for a week. 'To eat fish curry.'

Her mother had spent the day getting her favourite food prepared. Her father was busy with his flowers, watering them, tending to them. He made a bouquet of fresh roses and presented it to his daughter.

She returned within a week.

'How long will Bunny baba stay in the hostel?' Sunita darted a look at her mistress, sitting down, as she brought tea.

'Five years.'

'And why does sahib go off so often?'

'His profession, Sunita!' Simran smiled feebly.

Water ran in the kitchen as Sunita soaped the cups and saucers. Lucky woman, Simran thought. She had her household chores to keep her busy.

Simran had to attend her nephew's birthday the next day. The party was hosted at Safdarjung officers' club. Handing over the gift, a tent house, she wished her nephew a happy birthday and pecked him on his cheeks.

The guests started filling in. They made small groups, joked and laughed.

They all assembled near the centre table, as Vicky cut the cake with the help of his mother.

'Where is Varun?' a few asked her.

'In London, for arbitration.' She said this repeatedly.

She did not have the cake. It had a lot of cream in it. She had fish cutlets. Coming originally from a river area, eating fish was in her blood.

'I have purchased some Madhubani paintings,' one of them nudged at Simran.

'Show me', she spoke, munching. She took Simran to her house nearby.

Simran liked the painting of a bride, sitting on the palanquin, held by four palanquin bearers. All the four were topless, in a *dhoti* and a *chaddar*. Two peacocks sat at the base, with a large flower at the centre. She wanted to see more paintings. She took down the name of the shop on a piece of paper.

They came back. Dinner was being served. Simran took chicken biryani and salads and sat in a corner. Everyone was in hurry to eat and go home. It was a Sunday and the next day was a working day. She had no school-going children. And none waited for her at home.

She was a bit late for her classes on Monday. A boy saw her on the corridor, and blushed. She gave him a bright smile. She remembered her son when she saw him. They must be almost the same age.

The boy stood, staring at her.

Classes went on, one after the other. Simran had only one free period.

Ms. Mishra, one of the teachers, was sitting in the Staff Room, mimicking. The chief minister of her state was her target. Ms. Mishra joked about all things connected with her state. She made fun of her state but was ready to scratch the face of anyone else who tried doing so.

Holding a small lantern in her hand, Ms. Mishra jumped onto a table and mimicked the present chief minister.

There was a roar of laughter.

'Back home, things are in a bad shape', she moaned.

'Businessmen, doctors, engineers, they are leaving the state. The unemployed youth are taking to the guns. The politicians are exploiting them, the kidnappers are given political protection.'

'Kidnapping is the only industry we are left with,' she lamented.

'What is his vote bank?' Simran was interested.

'Muslim - Yadav combine. Though others are making a dent into it,' Ms. Mishra looked animated.

The bell rang and they dispersed.

Simran entered her classroom, sat on the edge of the table, and crossing one leg over the other, spoke. She delivered a lecture on federalism and powers of centre vis-a-vis the constituent states. The students took down notes.

'Unlike the US, we are part unitary, part federal,' she spoke. 'The states are not vested with the immense powers bestowed on American constituent states. But being a democracy with strong foundations, powers at both the levels are expected to remain within the limits assigned to them.'

The class was over. She went to watch a movie with Ms. Mishra in the nearby multiplex.

'How old are your children?' she enquired.

'One is five and the other seven.'

They sat munching popcorn.

Simran talked of her boredom. Ms. Mishra suggested she take up some course to keep herself occupied.

'That will also help boost your career.'

Simran could not sleep the whole night. She kept thinking. She got up, switched on the computer and started surfing the internet. She went to www.federalism.ch, looking for some summer university that would offer a short course.

Last year when her aunt had come to Delhi after doing a short course in Switzerland, she had given the URL to her. Simran had been quite impressed by her aunt at that time.

'Why don't you too try for it?' her aunt had said, scribbling the URL in Simran's thick, black diary, in her long, slanting hands.

There was a Swiss University that offered such courses. She did not want to go that far. She would rather go to some part of the country. Chennai. That was the place. She would consult her colleagues for she remembered distinctly that one of them had gone to Chennai last year.

She spent the next few days procuring forms, and filling them up. She seemed to be on a mission. At times she skipped her lunch, in search of more and more information.

Varun had come back. And he was busy. When he had time, he would learn yoga from Swami Ramdev.

Simran received a short, crisp letter from Chennai.

She read and re-read it, and then handed it over to Varun.

'Are you sure you want to go?'

'I need to get away,' Simran murmured.

'How long have we been married?'

'Twenty years.'

'Varun, when I am not here, will Swati shift in?'

'She is an efficient junior, and that is it,' he averted his eyes.

'I look old with lines on my face.'

'You still look ravishing.'

'I am not attractive.'

'Passersby still turn back to look at you.'

'What about you? You don't show interest in me any longer. Does Swati have a beautiful body?'

Varun lighted a cigarette. His wife was looking at him with stormy eyes. He had not seen her so restless all these years. Why don't women realize that men are by nature polygamous? And if some woman is willing to play the ball, why not? Nature has made us that way.

He had touched Swati on several occasions. Once, as she bent over one of her briefs making notes, Varun had come from behind and had removed her thick glasses. Suman and Atishi, his other juniors, had gone to the court. He had asked Swati to stay back and prepare notes in a matter she was required to argue.

Swati had simply looked at him. She asked no questions. He sat on his chair, taking Swati along with him. Putting his arms around her waist, he kissed her lightly on her hair. The pressure of her body maddened him. He touched her all over, unbuttoning her shirt. Swati reciprocated. Ummmm. He did not know that this young woman, hardly out of her teens, could be so interesting. She was rubbing herself against him. Simran had not given him such pleasure for years. Sex had become a mechanical thing for them.

Varun ensured that he took Swati along with him wherever he went. Swati's career progressed rapidly. She was getting cases in the early years of her career.

When they went to London, Varun had booked a single room for both of them. So his wife was aware of all this, he thought. He was curious to know who had told her all this. He lighted another cigarette.

'Relax Simran,' he laughed. 'Don't listen to what others say. It is all hogwash.'

'You have not answered me yet. Does Swati have a beautiful body?'

Varun remained silent. Swati's belly was flat, like the tabletop.

'So you are determined about going?'

'Yes.'

'I have applied for one year's leave. I may get the approval within a week.'

'O.K.'

Varun was buoyant.

One full year with Swati. What more could he ask for?

Simran dressed up to go to her college. She was in purple chiffon, her forearms with colourful bangles. Big, silver earrings shuddered as she walked. Her lips were painted a bright purple.

Varun said he would drop her. She sat beside her husband, her hands on her lap.

She looked at her husband furtively. She wondered if he loved her any more.

They stopped before the college gate, surrounded by a thick clump of trees. Boys and girls moved around, in small groups. Some wished her as she passed by.

Bunny rang up. She unzipped her purse, grabbed the phone, and shouted, 'Hello, how are you? Do you eat well? Is your roommate nice to you?'

'Don't worry, mamma,' he shouted, 'I am a big boy now. Take care of yourself.'

'Do hand over the phone to your friend. I want to know whether you eat well or not.'

'Ma, I will call up later,' saying so, he hung up hurriedly.

Simran entered the classroom, smiling wryly.

That night she had a bad dream.

'Get up Varun,' she started shaking him. He opened his eyes, throwing an irritated look at his wife. Simran said nothing. Varun got up, fumbled for his spectacles, and switched on the lights.

'Now what is your problem? No one is in the room, except for the two of us.'

Emboldened, as the room was flooded with light, she looked around. Varun was right. No one was around.

She left her room, and walked up to her terrace.

It was four in the morning. There was death-like silence outside. Long, thick trees, bathed in park lights, stood in the corner. Simran could not sleep. She was unhappy. They had worked hard, Varun had made a pile of money, but she was getting less and less happy.

A few generations ago, women were old enough to die at her age. Simran had no intention to die. And she wanted to live with a peaceful mind.

The greyish-white stones they had carried from Rishikesh shone in her flower pots. A dog writhed, as it lay on its back. She wondered if the animals had the same kind of feelings human beings had. Was the dog happy? Right now her only concern was, did the dog feel the same kind of turbulence as she felt? She felt a strange camaraderie with the dog.

Leave was sanctioned to her. She read the contents of the terms with a heavy heart. She looked at the house she had stayed in for twenty years.

Varun came home, blaring his horn. The guard sitting outside ran to open the gate. Varun poured whisky for himself. He looked old. Simran asked him to stop after he had had three pegs. His mobile rang continuously. Irritated, he bent and switched off the instrument. He hated it when the clients rang up after ten in the evening or before ten in the morning.

Dinner was served. Simran told him her leave had been sanctioned. She showed the letter from Chennai. He looked at it, nodded and went off to sleep.

She talked to her son. She knew he studied till late at night. She talked for a long time. The son listened patiently, encouraging his mother, urging her to take the plunge.

When the whole world slept, they talked to one other.

7

Chennai

The foundation of the modern city of Chennai was laid by M/s Cogan and Day, who set up a trading settlement in the fishing village of Chennaipatnam in 1639. This place was chosen by East India Company as the centre of their commercial activities in the South. Chennai has wide, clean roads, ancient temples, and beaches. Jaikumaran, the famous actor, never entered Chennai before taking rounds of an ancient temple he went to for worship. Simran too went inside the temple. She took flowers for offering.

Simran removed her slippers, and prostrated. She was told women did not prostrate the way she did.

'You can wear the flowers in your hair,' a local friend who had come along, suggested. Thousands of worshippers went inside the temple, bare-footed.

'In Mumbai Ganesh is the ruling deity but here, in Chennai, we revere his brother, Kartikeya,' he added.

'Some view these temples with the interest of a tourist,' he looked with disgust, 'but those who come with a feeling of reverence are rewarded.' Simran looked at herself. She was wearing jeans and T-shirt. She threw a look at him, searching for anger in his eyes. They proceeded towards the inner chambers of the temple, the sanctum sanctorum. All the worshippers stood in a row, their hands folded, as the head priest blew the conch shell. Simran covered her head with a handkerchief.

It was late in the evening when she came back. She had checked into a hotel, overlooking the sea. Thanking her friend at the porch, she came inside, and took her bath. She wore a pink nightdress, with white laces.

Pouring a drink in a tall glass, she carried it to the balcony. She pulled a chair and sat on it.

It was the month of June. She sat there, cross-legged, watching the waves.

She was inebriated after the two pegs. She went to the washroom, opening its door with misty eyes. She returned to the balcony. The waves looked more beautiful, the sea noisier. She sat there for hours. Like the sea which was answerable to none, Simran felt she was a free woman.

Tomorrow she would go to the faculty and enquire about the boarding facilities. She would not think of anything right now.

A boy came to her room, making enquiries about dinner. She dismissed him.

She bolted the door. She hit a table as she walked back, and fell on the floor. She slept on the floor the whole night.

Her friend came over the next evening. They drove to Marina Beach. Four and a half kilometre long, it is the second longest beach in the world, and one of the loveliest. 'Shall we go into the sea?' one of children walking on the beach asked her sister imploringly.

Simran was warned that the sea in those parts was violent. No one swam there. Women and children could be seen washing their hands and feet in water.

The entire evening was spent in roaming around, as she moved from one place to another, feeling Chennai, and savouring it. Water was scarce; people carried and stored it in colourful plastic pitchers.

They also went to Mahabalipuram, also known as Mamallapuram. Simran bought some rock figurines which she would keep in her hostel room. Away from daily worries of managing the household, she felt free. She climbed onto the rocks, went to one temple after the other. They had coconut water.

They came to a restaurant. Simran had onion *uthappam,* her friend *masala dosa.* It was cool inside, as the air conditioner droned in the background. She sat eating, dipping her *uthappam* in *sambhar* and *chutney.*

'When do your classes begin?'

'Tomorrow.'

'Do you like Chennai?'

'Oh yes.'

She came back to Chennai exhausted, had a glass of cold water, and went off to sleep.

Her current roommate was a slender lady, with closely cropped hair. Every day Simran found her going off with a young man in the evening, soon after they had tea.

'My Indian mentality compels me to ask you this question,' Simran said, as she looked at the comely face of the girl, young enough to be her daughter, 'are you serious about him?'

Mary, her roommate, smiled.

'Look, you are in a strange land living with strange people. You should not allow anyone to exploit you,' Simran would sit and advise as Mary lay on her bed, smiling. At times Simran felt Mary made fun of her in her absence.

One evening they decided to go for a concert. Mary had an ear for music, she moved slightly to and fro, swaying, absorbing the notes. Simran watched her intently. God had not given her the gift of singing.

Mary was different. Not only did she sing well, she danced well too. Her body had a flexibility which few have. But she was very fussy. Most of the time she skipped breakfast.

'Who is going to have these potatoes with such a thin gravy?' was her perpetual complaint. At night she would bring her pocket transistor close to her ears and listen to songs.

During hot and humid nights, Simran got restless. She would go to the bathroom, and start pouring water over her body. She would come back, without wiping herself dry. It felt cool as water evaporated, with the fan whirring above. When she could not sleep, she would go to the balcony.

When Mary laid curled on her bed, sleeping, Simran would put a sheet to cover her; Mary would relax and spread out her legs wide. At times Simran would make the notes and Mary would copy them.

The young lady was busy with her friend. Her concentration in studies slackened. She would attend her classes, come back, wear fresh clothes, and throw her discarded things on her bed. Simran would then spend at least half an hour arranging her clothes, and cleaning her bed. With passage of time, Simran started taking all this as part of her daily duties.

At regular intervals she talked to her husband and her son. They were all busy with their lives. She received her bank draft, which Varun would send in the first week of every month. She indulged herself the day she received the money. Mary and she would skip the dinner in the college hostel and go to a restaurant, where they would have chicken and butter *naan*. Mary would make it a point to thank Simran on such occasions. Simran would show mock anger and say, 'C'mon, you do not need to be so formal.'

One day both of them decided to go to see the sea lions. They bought tickets, had popcorn, and waited on stairs for the show to begin. There were rows of chairs on both sides.

The sea lions roared, and showed their skills. After each game, the trainer would throw a handful of fish at them. There was instant reward.

She had tried the same trick with her son during his admission in school. She remembered pacing up and down, waiting for their turn. And after each interview, she would drive down to McDonald's or Pizza Hut.

'You answer the questions you are asked, and we will immediately go for a treat,' she held out this promise every time her son had to be interviewed. The trick had worked. Bunny got a call from almost all the schools for admission.

After the show was over, the owner gave an account of how difficult it was to maintain those sea lions, and made a request for liberal donation.

It was three months since she had come to Chennai. She went to Delhi for a few days for Dussehra vacations. Mary stayed back.

Delhi was pleasant. It was cooler. There was a nip in the air in the morning. Simran went for morning walks with her husband. They would feel the chill in the mornings but soon they warmed up. Bunny had not come. He said he had his semester, and he needed to work. Sunita was happy that her mistress had come home.

'Sunita,' one day Simran accosted her maid, 'what was Sahib's routine when I was not here?'

'He was hardly at home,' Sunita said quietly.

'Sahib normally came back late at night. He drank heavily, had a light dinner, and went off to sleep.'

'Did anyone come along with him?'

'At times I have seen a lady come with Sahib.'

'But she never enters the house. The driver drops her back.' Sunita was busy dusting the chairs.

'Does she wear glasses?'

'Yes.'

'The thick ones?'

Sunita nodded, shuffling her feet.

'Sometimes Sahib would not come back at all. I would keep waiting for him for hours, sleeping on floor. But he would not come back. Normally he would be back the next day, early in the morning.'

Sunita was not looking at her mistress.

'He would dress up, ask me to lay his breakfast on the table, and hurry off.'

'Why don't you come back, Memsahib?'

'Nine more months and I will be back.'

'Men are like horses, they need to be reined in.' Sunita went back to her kitchen, feeling safe and secure. She answered Simran's questions reluctantly.

Simran went back to Chennai. Mary said she had missed her. Scores of discarded clothes lay on the bed. There was a thick layer of dust on the study table. Mary looked at Simran and smiled sheepishly. Simran decided to clean the room after she had taken her breakfast. She would clean up the entire place before she took bath.

The classes resumed. They were to prepare for the quarterly assessment. They had to work hard for it. Life was hectic. Simran prepared notes for Mary and herself. Mary hardly studied.

'You are young,' Simran would tell her, 'you need to work to build your career.'

'All this you can do later,' she would say, pointing towards her friend's motorcycle that he had parked outside the faculty. Mary would smile, and go away. Simran would look exasperated as the motorcycle fumed, and disappeared from sight.

The quarterly assessment was done. She presented her paper and scored the highest marks. All her class fellows started pestering her for treat. Mary got a box of sweets, popped one in her own mouth, and passed the box to the others. Simran promised to take them for treat the next day.

'Why do you need to work so hard?' Mary questioned her one day, as they sat on the study table.

'Because I need to feel useful.'

'You have everything in life, why do you need to slog?'

Mary's father was dead. Her brother paid for her education, and she desperately wanted to be independent and to relieve her brother of her burden. An additional qualification would have helped her.

Mary did not know that when one is Simran's age, one needs to rediscover oneself.

Mary was young. She had the whole world to look forward to. Her immediate concerns were to get a husband, and a job. She failed to understand how a woman as affluent and secure as Simran could be unhappy.

'Had I been in your place, I would have splurged and sat at home, contentedly,' Mary would say, as they lay on their beds, looking at ceiling. Simran would think of Varun and herself, when they were young.

Mary would think of her friend and dream of a small house in which the two of them would live.

If her friend had a job, it would have been easier. Every time Mary coaxed him to apply for a job, he would smile, and change the topic. At times Mary felt like leaving him. If he did not have a sense of responsibility, he did not deserve her. He would drink and look into her eyes, and say he loved her. But that would not suffice, Mary would say.

Simran would read her newspaper sitting on bed. Mary, when she got hold of the newspaper, ensured that it became crumpled by the time she was finished with it. Simran would rearrange the pages.

Simran normally wore *sarees* when she went to attend her classes. In the evenings she wore jeans and T-shirts. She would apply light makeup, hire a cab, and go to Marina Beach. She would sit on the beach for hours, watching the waves toss under black sky. She would start walking from one end to the other, her jeans rolled up to her knees. She became a regular fixture on the beach. A solitary figure, walking among waves. She would come back, her clothes coated with sand. She would go to the bathroom immediately, throw the pair of jeans in the bucket and then turn on the tap. In the morning, she would wash it with soap and water.

Simran knew what she had missed in Delhi. The sea beckoned her, and the urge was to come back, again and again. Simran would carry sheets of paper and pen to the seashore. She would sit, putting her thoughts on paper. She would write letters to her husband and son. She sat, writing, watching the sun disappear. Like a sage she sat in isolation, oblivious of noise all around her, as the sky turned orange and then black. She would then fold the papers carefully, put them in her large shoulder bag, and lie down, staring at the sky. The stars, the moon, and noisy sea–all this took her to a different world. She felt closer to God and His gifts.

Six months passed. Chennai had become second home to her.

Almost half of the course was over. In six months she would be back in Delhi, doing what she had been doing for years. Occasionally she received Sunita's letter.

'Things are not the same after Bunny baba and you left. Sahib behaves strangely. Are you happy, Memsahib? I am not. This is my family, and I will live here till my last breath.

'Please come back,' she would conclude.

Simran would smile, fold the letter carefully, and put it in her drawer. Sunita does not know about the kind of contentment she felt these days. I will come back, she would write, where else will I go?

Varun wanted to know if Simran would come to Delhi for her Christmas vacations. She wrote back she had not decided.

'Mary has invited me to her home for Christmas vacations,' she had written, 'I may not get another such opportunity.'

Mary was chirpy. 'It will be great. We shall have great fun together.'

They started packing. Simran decided to take all her *sarees*. Who knows, if they were a conservative family, they may not like her wearing western dresses.

Simran went to the Mall to buy gifts for her family members. She took Mary along. What colour did her mother like? Did her sister like wearing skirts? How about a shirt for her brother?

'Mary, what will you like for a Christmas gift?'

'A nice, embroidered *saree*. The kind of *saree* you wear.'

Simran got a beautiful *saree* embroidered. The man took more than a fortnight to complete the work.

'It is supposed to be a Christmas gift,' she would remind, 'and I want it soon.'

When the *saree* was finally delivered, she kept it in a bag, along with her other gifts.

8

Passion

Varun looked at Swati work in the kitchen.

Piling a few pillows on top of one another, he lay down.

He picked up a book. He read for an hour. He got up, looked out of the window.

It was a hot and humid day. He opened a bottle of vodka, and made a large drink. He felt buoyant as alcohol spread in his body. He started rubbing his face with his fingers. He looked at Bunny's photograph, on the study table. He was in his nappy, hardly six months old. Varun smiled.

Swati made a lot of noise in the kitchen. She chopped vegetables, fried them. She made rapid movements, working with dexterity. Varun looked at her lazily.

Drunk, he got up and switched on the television. A young reporter, in a crisp cotton suit, spoke excitedly.

Bunny called up. 'I am fine, Papa,' he said.

Leaning against a chair, he tried getting up. He staggered. A book fell on the table. Varun stooped to pick it up.

He looked out of the window. It rained outside.

When he turned back, he saw Swati stand behind him. She had brought a chilled bottle of water, and a bucket of ice.

Varun looked at Swati. Her cleavage was visible. He was turned on. Varun caught hold of her hand. There was thirst in her eyes. He made a swift movement, pressing her against the wall. She let out a cry. There was an oily patch on the wall.

Picking up his half-filled glass, he pulled Swati nearer; he pressed the glass against her lips.

Swati made a face, drops of alcohol trickled down her chin. Varun snatched the glass back and took a large sip. He rubbed his cheeks against Swati's.

Swati fell on the floor. She got up after a while, and went to the kitchen.

Varun made another drink for himself. Water splashed as he dropped cubes of ice.

He walked to the kitchen. He lifted her, and sat her on the kitchen slab. Swati sat still.

Varun kissed her passionately. The doorbell rang. Varun frowned. A boy had come to deliver a box of pineapple pastries.

9

Sothavilai

Simran and Mary reached Sothavilai, a village in the Kanyakumari district of Tamilnadu. Sothavilai is only six hundred metres away from seashore. They reached there early in the morning, around 6 a.m. Mary's brother William was at the bus stand to receive them. Hauling Mary's bag on his shoulders, he led the way as Simran wheeled her suitcase. William drove quietly. The cross dangling in his neck swayed as the car moved with speed. William did not talk much. Simran tried guessing his age. Maybe he was thirty-two, or thirty. He had a mole on his chin. He had a wheatish complexion and was of medium height.

William parked the car in a small garage they had built outside their house. Mary jumped off the car, almost dragging Simran along with her, leaving William to take care of the baggage. Simran was introduced to the family. Mary's mother was an old lady. Her sisters, Matilda and Agnes were short, and as chirpy as Mary was. Matilda was married last year. She had come to her mother's home for her delivery. She waddled around the home in a shapeless nightie; her face had a glow seen on a pregnant woman's face.

Agnes was twelve, and spent her days playing when she came back from school. William was the breadwinner. He was not married. His deep eyes spoke a silent language.

Mary had told her that their father had died when William was seventeen. He had taken a part-time job and completed his studies.

'I have never seen my brother do things other boys do,' Mary told her. 'When his friends moved around with girls, my brother worked. His youth was lost in taking care of us.'

William lived in a small room in the house. It was barely furnished, with a small bed, a study table, and a chair. He was fond of reading; his bookshelf stacked with writings on Marx and Marxism. After dinner, he went to his room, switched on the table lamp and read for at least two to three hours.

It was almost a week since Simran had come to Mary's home. They celebrated Mary's homecoming. William looked at Simran when she handed over his cake to him. His eyes contained a certain pain. Simran smiled. For a change Matilda was in a *saree*. All the three sisters wore flowers in their hair. Mary's mother looked the happiest. Her children were home. She looked at Simran fondly and made enquiries about Mary. Simran gave indulgent replies.

William looked at his sisters indulgently as they sang, danced and had fun. Simran wondered how anyone could be so quiet. Simran felt William stared at her. Her cheeks reddened. They had fun till late at night. William retired to his room, holding a book in his hand. Simran shared the room with Mary and Matilda. Agnes slept with her mother.

In Sothavilai, there are natural sand dunes about fifty to sixty feet high, between the village and the sea. These are covered with trees, providing natural protection to the village from the sea.

Simran liked Sothavilai. Mary went to meet her co-villagers. She took Simran along with her. 'This woman from Delhi is beautiful,' an old woman remarked, as she caressed Simran on her cheeks. It had been ages she had received a compliment.

They met more people. Many of them praised Simran for her long, pointed nose and pink lips.

When they came back, it was dark. William was in the kitchen, preparing *masala dosa*. He loved cooking.

Simran entered the kitchen. William placed *masala dosa* on a plate, and offered it to Simran. Simran took a bite. It was tasty. Suddenly she had the impulse to sit on the kitchen slab and eat. Simran looked at William. His unshaven face had stubble. He put another *dosa* on her plate.

'No, I don't want more,' she protested.

'I have prepared this especially for you,' he said.

Simran tossed and turned on her bed that night. Matilda lay on her side, her stomach sticking out. Mary slept. Simran got up and walked up to the verandah. She found William sitting on a wooden chair, looking at the lonely road.

'It is hot inside. I couldn't sleep.' she offered explanation.

Simran pulled a chair and sat down. They did not speak much. After about half an hour, she got up and said she was going to her room. William switched on the light as Simran crossed the verandah and re-entered her room. The lights were switched off as she shut the door. William had touched her lightly. She shivered.

Simran got up at four in the morning. She did not know what was happening to her. Whenever she tried to sleep, the face of William appeared before her eyes. She rebuked herself. What was she thinking? She was on the wrong side of thirties and William must be in his early thirties. She tried to dismiss those thoughts from her mind.

Sothavilai is a small village. The village adjoining Sothavilai is a village of fishermen. Occasionally William would go with them, and fish. His friends among the fishermen were all jovial. They slapped William on his thighs, as William sat, very silent. They all loved William; not only because they admired William but also because they knew they could trust him.

Simran entered William's room to get something to read for herself. William's bed was littered with his clothes and books. Simran picked up the books, and started arranging them on the bookrack. She picked up one of his T-shirts. She smelled it. She felt she was smelling him. As if in slow motion, she picked up all his dresses, and set them in hangers. She smoothened the crumpled bed sheet.

Mary entered the room.

'I felt like reading something', she said quietly.

Simran picked up a book.

'Don't read that!' Mary said, 'it is one of those books on Marx, William never tires of reading.'

'I will sit here and read for sometime,' Simran said. 'I will join you for tea.'

Mary left the room. William's room was dark. Simran switched on the table lamp, and sat on the chair. She opened the book, a thick, bound volume, and started flipping through its pages. 'If William likes Marx, I will also like him', she decided.

Then she saw William had scribbled something on the margins. William had expressed his love for some lady living in the neighbourhood. Simran felt jealous. She had not felt as jealous when she came to know of her husband's escapades. The woman in thick glasses, back home, did not give her the heartache she felt when she read William's outpourings, expressing his sentiments for another woman. She went to the bathroom, and turned on the tap. She did not know what was happening to her. This man, whom she had hardly known for a few days, was giving her such pain.

She went to her room, and hid her face in her pillow.

'Leave her alone,' the old lady was telling her daughters, 'she is missing her home. Let her cry. She will feel lighter.'

Simran fell into a light slumber.

When Simran got up, it was dark. She recollected what had happened, everything coming back to her in slow motion. Then she felt light. Life is short. Don't waste it. She went for a stroll with Mary.

'Mary, I want to go to the children's park,' Simran said. Simran got onto one of the swings, and placing her feet firmly on the ground, she gave a kick. She went up, reaching the sky. 'Mary, look at this,' Simran was shouting happily, her face turned towards heaven. Life is beautiful, she thought.

'Let us go back,' she told Mary. Mary looked at her. Something was hurting Simran, she knew. She had known Simran for the past six months and she understood her.

'Why doesn't Bunny ring up?' Mary asked Simran.

'He is busy with his studies.' Simran gave an abrupt reply.

Mary did not probe further.

Simran always felt William looked at her face, her body.

The following day they decided to go for a picnic. Mary's mother got up early in the morning, and packed vegetable sandwiches, some napkins, and water. They went to a nearby lake.

Agnes ran around. She played cricket with William and Mary. Simran also joined them. Matilda and her mother sat on the ground.

It was time for refreshments. They made a semicircle, the plates were placed before them. Mary served sandwiches, patties and other goodies. Her mother handed over the glasses to them. Suddenly the sky darkened and black clouds clung to the sky. They removed their things quickly and ran towards shelter. There were small, hut-like enclosures built at regular intervals. They went to one such shelter for protection. Another family was already sitting there. They put their things on benches placed on side. Rain drops fell on Simran's hands as she stood near the benches. The black sky filled her with a strange sensation. She could feel a change in herself. She felt she was desired, and that made her buoyant.

The sky cleared and they left the shelter. Simran walked up to the rose bushes. She stooped, smelling a large, pink rose. She had a sudden impulse to pluck it and give it to William. She looked around her. William was running with Agnes. Agnes clutched life in her two little hands. Simran walked up to them. Agnes caught hold of Simran's hand and started moving in a circle, pulling Simran along with her. Her hands were outstretched, and she laughed. Her eyes shone. William saw Simran, the *pallu* of her *saree* swaying in the gentle breeze.

Matilda was sitting with her mother under a tree. She sat and talked to her mother about her husband and her annoying in-laws. Matilda cribbed about them.

'Take care,' her mother warned her, 'you need to be cheerful at this time. Don't let all this affect your baby.'

Matilda's eyes shone as her gaze travelled to the swell of her belly.

Simran rubbed her eyes as she woke up the next day, early in the morning. Her mobile phone rang. There were five missed calls. It was Bunny.

'I am speaking from a guest house near Jim Corbett Wild Life Sanctuary', he was shouting.

'When did you reach there?' Simran was aghast. 'Don't you need to inform us about anything?' she admonished him.

'I informed Papa on phone, he said I could go.'

'Mamma, it is great fun,' Bunny sounded excited. 'Yesterday I saw a tiger, its eyes shone as it hid in the Valley, near the water source, waiting for the deer to come in search of water.'

Simran poured a cup of tea for herself. She listened drowsily. 'Our driver is a local and he knew where to find the tiger. He brought us to a desolate spot late at night. We waited, with the car lights switched off, as the tiger walked right up to our car and then headed towards the water hole.'

'Ma, it is great fun.'

'O.K.', Simran continued. 'But be very careful. When you are inside the jungle, do not get down from the jeep, wild animals get disturbed. And ask your driver to drive slowly.'

'And wear thick shoes,' saying so, Simran hung up.

She could feel the rush of adrenaline when one is ball to ball with a tiger or a leopard. Simran knew of a small village in the midst of a jungle where children walked for three-four kilometres daily to go to their school. They played with tigers, she was told, just as the others did with their dogs.

Simran felt a certain uneasiness. A part of her, she felt, was linked to Sothavilai. The thought of leaving it saddened her. Sothavilai was a soothing balm to her. It was a feeling she had experienced after a long time.

She put on her spectacles and started writing on sheets with concentration. She studied for close to three hours. Her mind was alert. By the time she finished, her table was full of sheets. Her hand ached.

She brushed and had her breakfast with Mary's mother. Mary took Simran to a nearby temple. She waited outside as Simran took a flight of steps. Simran rang the big bell that hung near the entrance.

'If you have any wish, the goddess will certainly fulfill it', the priest was saying. 'People from distant villages come to pray in this temple.' Simran covered her head and sat on her knees. Her eyes were shut and hands folded. The priest applied *tilak*, a mixture of vermilion and rice, on Simran's forehead. On their way back, Simran and Mary halted at Mary's friend's for a cup of tea.

On Christmas, they woke up early. Mary found her gift on her bed, under the pillow. William had got the Christmas tree which Agnes was busy decorating. The bells, the stars, the chocolates, they shone as Agnes fixed them up, one by one. Mary's mother and Matilda were busy in the kitchen. Simran had baked a large cake for them. She went with them to the church.

'I will prepare breakfast today,' she announced, as she tucked the *pallu* of her *saree*, and proceeded to the kitchen. Mary's family sat on dining chairs, encouraging Simran to prepare something typical of North.

'Mary, come and help me,' Simran called from the kitchen.

Mary ran, her hands covered with soil. She had been tending to the plants they kept on the verandah. Mary laid the table, putting the bowl containing the *chhole* at the centre.

'It was a delicious breakfast,' Mary's mother remarked, washing her hands in the washbasin. She removed the *chhole* that had been clogging the washbasin. Mary's mother was a satisfied woman.

They organized a small show. A ten-year old child danced to the tune of the latest Hindi numbers as the audience clapped. Mary mimicked, she was good at it. William sang in his deep-throated voice, his eyes searching Simran as he rendered the notes. Matilda was busy serving the snacks, moving in slow paces. She looked completely round. Some children from the neighbourhood also performed a group dance.

During evening, they sat near the Christmas tree and chatted. Agnes had worn the red and white robes of Santa Claus and she ran around the house, the bell tinkling in her hands. They laughed as Agnes gave chocolates to each one of them. Mary's mother was busy preparing the dinner.

Mary, Agnes, William and Simran went out for a short walk. Matilda helped her mother. Agnes ran around, with Mary following her. Simran and William walked slowly, close to each other. They continued walking silently. Simran looked ahead of her. Agnes and Mary were not to be seen anywhere. William came closer to Simran; she could almost smell him. He took her hand. Simran looked at William. There was passion in his eyes.

Simran started searching for Agnes and Mary. They were behind a thick clump of trees, the foliage bright and new. Simran joined them. William sat nearby, his back turned towards them. While Agnes spoke hurriedly, Mary looked at her sister wistfully. Very soon, she would be back in Chennai, and miss Agnes.

'Simran, shall we pack up this brat and take her along with us?' Mary's eyes twinkled as she looked at Agnes.

'Good idea,' Simran said, 'and we can take turns looking after her.'

'No', Agnes protested, 'what about my school, my friends, and my mother?'

'And what if William goes along with you?' Simran asked.

William looked back.

'Well, that is different,' Agnes had her hand on her chin. 'I will consult mother and tell you.'

'Don't rack your brains,' Simran ruffled the child's hair, 'let us go home.'

It was a cheerful dinner. The big star William had hung outside the house swayed as wind blew. Specks of light peeped through its pores.

Mary's mother offered her prayers and thanked God for everything.

'My husband loved this day,' she was telling Simran, tear trickling down. He spent days in advance, preparing for Christmas. He was the happiest when he gave gifts to children and cut the cake for them.' She looked at her children with some pride.

'I don't remember exactly when William slipped into his father's shoes. The burden of the family was thrown on him at an early age, but look at the way he has carried it.'

'His father must be looking from there,' she looked up, towards the sky, 'and must be proud of such a son.'

'Why did William not marry?' Simran was hardly audible.

'He loved a girl who stayed in the neighbourhood. Her family shifted to the United States. She went with them. I have heard the girl has already been married twice, and is the mother of three children.'

Simran rose. When she went to her room she found Matilda flat on the bed, her legs spread out. She was groaning. Simran sat near her and started massaging her legs. Matilda liked it. Simran continued for about half an hour till Matilda fell into a gentle sleep. Simran went to the bathroom and turned on the shower. She felt exhilarated as water streamed down her hair, her nose, and her chest. She sat under the shower, her head between her legs, as she soaked herself in water. She remembered the stories she had heard of past life. Did she have an association with this family and Sothavilai in her past life?

Mary banged at the door.

'You will catch a cold,' she shouted.

Simran emerged, her hair wrapped in a striped towel.

10

The Younger Man

After dinner, Simran went to William's room. She looked for something light to read. She took a novel, and read the review, given at the back. The novel seemed interesting. She read for more than two hours. It was a gripping tale, and she read on.

It was late at night when William came home. He had had his dinner with his friends. His mother opened the door and went back to her room. She was half asleep. His sisters were sleeping in their own room.

As William opened the door, he saw Simran bend over a book. He stood before her, his eyes fixed on Simran.

Simran looked up. As she was leaving the room, William caught her. He bolted the door and threw Simran on the rug.

William disrobed her. Simran did not resist. Then slowly he removed his track pants and T-shirt. He started rubbing his bare body against Simran's. He cupped her breasts, then bit them. Simran moaned as he started kissing her feet, her legs.

He cupped her hips, stroking it. Simran's hair was long. It covered her back, reaching right up to her hips. William rolled her hair, and kissed her on her forehead. Simran clung to him.

William stopped. He could hear someone open the refrigerator. It was Matilda. She was pregnant, and needed to eat something. After a while, it was quiet.

He looked at Simran, who had wrapped the bedcover over her bare body. He removed the cover, took her on his lap.

Simran stroked William as he held her in the crook of his arms. Simran let out a muffled cry. With that cry, the pain of rejection went out of her system.

Simran left the room stealthily. She went to the washroom and washed herself.

She tiptoed to her room. Mary and Matilda slept peacefully. The younger woman was curled up. Simran covered her with the sheet. Mary turned around, and spread out her legs and went off to sleep.

Simran lay beside her.

Matilda opened her eyes. She had seen Simran emerge out of her brother's room.

One day Mary's mother asked Simran, 'Does Mary study hard?'

There was a glint in Simran's eyes. 'Shall I tell you the truth?'

'When will she understand her brother needs to be relieved of his responsibilities?'

'Don't worry. Your daughter knows what she is doing.'

Simran smiled as she saw Mary, her hands on her hips, her eyebrows raised.

'Try to understand,' she was telling Mary later on. 'Your mother has gone through a bad phase. She needs to relax.'

'I hope you have not told her about my young man?'

'Who?' Simran feigned ignorance.

Mary glared at her.

'O.K. O.K.', she laughed, 'I have not told her about him.'

Matilda entered the room, her hands coated with flour.

'Does the young man know you are such a horrible cook?'

'Learn cooking from your brother,' Simran suggested.

Matilda looked at her.

Simran averted her eyes.

'William cooks well, does it effortlessly,' Simran explained, her eyes fixed on her fingers. William had kissed her fingers, her hands, her lips.

During evening they watched a movie on the television. William was sprawled on the couch. Mary lay on the carpet, her hands cupping her cheeks. Others sat on the sofa.

Simran felt William looked at her. She fervently hoped his sisters had not seen him. After about half an hour, William left the room.

'What a boring movie!' Mary yawned, looking at the ceiling.

Simran nodded. Her thoughts were elsewhere.

Mary changed the channel.

They had an early dinner. Matilda laid the table, walking funnily from one side to the other. They ate silently.

'One more,' Agnes said, as her mother served.

When Simran was washing her hands, William came close to her. He whispered, 'Come to my room after sometime.'

Simran looked at him.

'I have bought some new novels,' he said aloud. 'Come and have a look.'

When Simran went to William's room, he was sprawled on his bed, reading the newspaper. Some books were scattered, all new and freshly bound. Simran sat at the edge.

'I thought you were interested in palmistry,' saying so, William pushed a book towards her.

'I have some knowledge in this field,' he continued, and started reading her palm.

'Your lines say you are in love with a man who lusts for you.'

Simran blushed.

William kissed her palm. Simran looked towards the door.

'Don't worry, no one comes to my room without knocking.'

She moved closer. William rubbed his cheeks against hers.

'Will you come to Chennai when I go back?'

'What will happen if your husband comes to know of all this?'

Simran thought of Swati and said, 'I don't care.'

When Simran went to her room, Matilda was sitting on the bed, eating an apple.

Their eyes met.

11

The Sea Rocks

It was December 26, 2004, the day after Christmas. At nine - thirty in the morning, they had breakfast. William's friend, Sekhar, came over and said that strange things were happening to the sea. The water was receding. People were rushing to the shore, as sea bed lay exposed, and fish could be seen without water. People were collecting fish hurriedly. Coral reef could be seen in sea bed.

Mary said she wanted to go to the seashore. They were all excited. The entire family got into the car. William parked the car on the sand dunes.

At eleven or so, they saw a series of waves coming towards them, fast. The waves came rapidly, one after the other. Water did not recede this time. People were thrown away as a wall of water, quite high, came towards them and beyond the sand dunes. Simran felt her feet being swept away as it engulfed her. She let out a loud cry. William, who was close to her, caught her by the arm. For a moment, the deafening sound of the sea numbed their senses. It was as if a huge dam had broken. William and Simran were thrown on a coconut tree. William held on to its leaves.

'Simran, give me your hand,' William shouted, as the sea roared. He held her hand tightly and pulled her up.

'Place your foot here,' he cried, as Simran tried climbing on to the tree. William left her hand as she got a foothold.

Then he came down, slowly, stretching his legs and planting them close to Simran's. He held her tightly. The deafening cries of people could be heard as waves charged ruthlessly. Simran was hysterical. She dug her nails into William's cheeks. She wanted to say something to William. She could not. She had lost her voice. William covered Simran's eyes with his hand, and with the other hand he stroked her hair. She looked up at William, her eyes filled with fear.

A woman, thrown on a coconut tree, had a puzzled look on her face.

Slowly water started receding. Its fury over, the sea was overcome with fatigue.

Agnes was dead. Her body had been thrown back. Their mother had held on to a tree for about two hours. She could not speak for a long time. Matilda's backbone had been hit and fractured. She lost her baby. Thirty people from Sothavilai lost their lives that day.

In the neighbouring village, inhabited by fishermen, about six hundred perished. Their boats were damaged, their nets washed away.

Many survived.

It was tsunami, ocean waves produced by earthquakes or underwater landslides.

When things were in control, William escorted Mary and Simran to Chennai. Chennai too had been badly hit by the tsunami.

It was feared that there would be outbreak of diseases like malaria, cholera, dengue fever. However, tsunami actually helped slow down the malaria, as mosquitoes cannot breed in brackish water.

William returned to Sothavilai after two days. His mother was grief-stricken, everything she touched reminded her of Agnes. She had not emptied her daughter's cupboard. Her dresses still hung there. Her box of clips and bands lay untouched. The old lady moved around the house like a ghost. Matilda was recuperating. She cried for her unborn child, and none had the heart to tell her that she would never become a mother.

William stood by his mother. At times the mother looked up, towards the sky, looking for support. She sat by Matilda all day long, tending to her, sharing her grief. Matilda's husband had come immediately on getting the information. She cried inconsolably as she saw him.

Matilda's husband sat beside his wife all day, comforting her. He was posted in Delhi. He had made frantic attempts to contact his wife in Sothavilai. He had sent his brother to Sothavilai to find out if things were alright. The moment he received the news of the tragedy that had struck his wife and her family, he had rushed to Sothavilai.

At night when the entire household slept, William read reports on tsunami.

William shut the book he was reading as Simran's face, horror-stricken, rose before his eyes. He could hear Agnes laugh.

'Help me go off to sleep,' she would demand, as she would pull William along with her.

He sobbed, burying his face in his hands. The girl in the neighbourhood had asked him to come along with her to the US. He had refused; he could not leave his family. He had consoled himself; so what if he was not happy? At least his family was happy.

William looked at his cross. Why me, Lord? He asked.

Simran talked to her husband on phone. The killer waves would have swept her away, she said, had Mary's brother William not come to her rescue.

At times Simran woke up in the middle of the night to find Mary crying. Mary sat up, her head in her hands, and cried. Both the women would cling to each other, comforting and consoling.

When Simran went to the Marina beach, she watched the waves curiously as they surged forth and receded. For thousands, life had taken a strange turn. She had heard the story of a man who had lost his family to the killer waves. He walked on the beach, day and night, waiting.

This is life. All of a sudden you are struck with such force that you stagger. But then as a fisherman had told Simran years ago, we are shameless. We do not take much time to foıget things.

When Simran was in Delhi, a bitch had given birth to four puppies in her garden. One day Simran called the gardener and asked him to take away the puppies. Every night, when Simran went to sleep, the bitch stood near her window, and moaned. Simran could not sleep. And then one day she saw the bitch giving birth to more puppies in her backyard; when Simran looked into the eyes of the bitch, she found hope.

Bunny's half yearly exams were over. He had done well.

Simran encouraged Mary to sing. 'God has given you a beautiful gift,' she would coax her, looking at her encouragingly. 'Why don't you release a music album? Singing would give you an outlet.'

'Look at the scores of music albums that are released every day. You are talented, you can do much better than many of them.' Mary would smile feebly.

Bunny came to Chennai to see his mother. Simran took him to Marina. He had read about the havoc wreaked, he was curious to go to the beach. Mother and son stayed on the beach till late in the evening.

'My mother is the most loving thing in this world,' Bunny looked at Simran endearingly, when she re-lived her experience at Sothavilai.

'Sothavilai is a small village,' Simran was telling him, 'and its inhabitants are nice people. You must come with me to Sothavilai one day.'

'I will show you the tree to which I clung for my life; had Uncle William not been there, your mother would have been no more.'

'I want to go there right now, Ma.'

'O.K., let me talk to Mary.'

The very next day, early in the morning, they set out for Sothavilai. Mary was keen to meet her family. Bunny wanted to see the place where his mother had almost lost her life.

William took them to the beach in his car. He parked it on the sand dunes, and started walking towards the beach. Others followed him. William stopped before a clump of trees and pointed towards the tree to which Simran and he had clung. Bunny took out his camera and shot photographs. William showed him the trees where a man had been jammed. He showed another one where a child had been thrown after his skull was smashed. Mary cried. Mary wondered what life had in store for her. She felt hers was a cursed family. God singles out her family and deals cruel blows to it, at regular intervals.

In the evening, William took Bunny to the village of fishermen. The fishermen were going through severe economic crisis. The survivors were luckless. William felt the dead were lucky enough to escape starvation. Bunny sat by old men, and comforting them, each one of them had a story to tell. When they came to know that Bunny was training to become a doctor, they said in one voice, 'Come to the village and open a dispensary.' Bunny was touched.

Simran was fond of her son. Tsunami had brought her closer to him. She had seen death from close quarters; she understood the value of life.

Simran took him to a saloon and forced him to get a haircut when they were back in Chennai. Mary had stayed back in Sothavilai. Simran took permission to keep her son in her room for a few days. Her son was taller than her, and she looked at him proudly as he walked with her.

By the time Simran finished with unpacking and cleaning the room, it was quite late. They went to a restaurant. North Indian food was more expensive in Chennai. They placed their order and waited. Simran saw a woman, her head shaven, a large *bindi* on her forehead, sitting on the table ahead of her. Bunny stared at her.

In Chennai, women could be spotted with their heads shaven. Getting their heads shaven by girls and boys was in fashion when she was in college; but she could not understand why orthodox - looking women shaved off their heads. Rajsekharan, who studied with her, told her that it was customary for men and women to offer their hair at Lord Balaji's shrine up on the Thirumala Hills near Tirupati in Andhra Pradesh. Men and women could be seen in rows, their heads bent, as the barbers did their job with lightning speed. The sale of hair was a great source of revenue for the temple authorities.

'I am starved,' he grumbled. 'It seems we will be the last ones to get something to eat.' They had ice cream after the meal. Banana split. Bunny licked away his ice cream bowl. He dug into Simran's ice cream. She had hardly taken a few bites and was not inclined to take more. Simran looked at him indulgently.

'I am full, I cannot walk', he said, standing up and putting the pressure of his body on the table.

They took a taxi back.

Simran got up at four in the morning and started studying. Bunny slept. His hands were on his chest. All of a sudden Simran stopped. She felt the waves surge towards her, and throw her away. Her feet dangled, and she held on to the tree. Simran's throat was parched. She poured a glass of water and gulped it down quickly. She envied Bunny who slept soundly, nothing bothering him.

Simran woke up Bunny. He rubbed his eyes and looked at his mother lazily. Simran could hardly sleep. She had another glass of water. She spoke incoherently. Bunny sat next to his mother.

'Don't worry Ma, it is all over,' he spoke. He saw dread on his mother's face.

The prospect of death is terrifying, and Bunny knew it. He saw it in his mother's eyes.

12

A New Chapter

Simran had completed her course. She did not want to return to Delhi. She wrote to her college authorities and requested them to transfer her to one of its branches in Chennai. They obliged her.

She took a small house on rent — a bedroom with attached bath, a small kitchen, and a study. The college was five minutes walk from her house. Her husband needed her no longer, and she did not care. In a few years, Bunny would be a doctor, she would then ask him to join her in Chennai, and start his private practice. One day Bunny would become a reputed doctor. Her son would make her proud of him. Sometimes she wondered if Varun missed her. He did call up, occasionally, telling her about friends, colleagues. Ms. Mishra's parents had shifted to Delhi. Both were doctors, and successful practitioners. They were tired of constant threats from criminals, seeking ransom, and decided to leave their state.

Cookie was put in a boarding school. Ms. Singh was concerned about Simran, Varun wrote, and wanted Simran to come back. Liar, she muttered. You do not want me back, nor do any one of those you have mentioned.

Simran lay on her bed, her head propped against two pillows, as these thoughts flitted across her mind. She would also think of William. Mary had left Chennai after her course was over, and they had lost touch. The thought of William brought back memories of pain and desire.

Once a while Simran missed Delhi. Janpath, where she loved to shop, the corners where she had egg rolls, and the plays they showed at Kamani. Simran missed the narrow lanes of Chandni Chowk, the Connaught Place and its long corridors with pillars. More than anything else, she felt the urge to speak in Hindi, the language they don't normally speak in Chennai.

It was a regulated life for Simran. She did not have time to think much during daytime but at night, when all slept, she felt frightened, insecure. Occasionally she sensed someone stood behind the curtains, it made her sit up all night. She would switch on the lights and sit and hold a magazine. Then she would fall asleep.

Simran feared life. It was scary and uncertain. She had suicidal tendencies; may be the other world would be kinder, and have less complications. When death had looked at her, straight into her eyes, she had fumbled. One jump into the turbulent sea, it would have rid her of all the pain. She had heard of wandering spirits of those who had had an unnatural death.

And mysteries fascinated her.

Death, mystery, and the other world notwithstanding, Simran found herself at the crossroad, not knowing where she was headed. A year ago everything was predictable - an early breakfast, a few lectures in the college, tea at home, and an early dinner. A son who was grown up, who shut himself in his room most of the time. Simran loathed it. There was no anticipation, no excitement, nothing unusual. At times she did hear about Varun and his junior. The thought of Varun ever leaving her did not cross her mind.

It was different now. She was not so sure Varun wanted her back. Why did he not oppose her when she announced she would take a transfer to Chennai? She had detected a hint of smile on his lips, a smile of relief.

'Take Sunita along with you,' he had recommended, 'she will help you set up your household there.'

'It would be convenient for you too,' she had muttered silently.

Simran was not one of those who would shout, rave and bang her head. She was financially independent; the last thing that she would do was to go to a man with a begging bowl.

'Please do not throw me out,' when she imagined herself saying these things, she cringed. Her sense of pride forbade her from saying so. Simran may not have been an ideal wife but her husband's well-being had been uppermost in her mind; and, more or less, she had been faithful to him.

Till she met William.

She picked up the *Times of India*, the national daily, in an attempt to divert her mind from unpleasant thoughts. The election results of a few states were given in a tabular form. The names of the parties and number of seats bagged was displayed. Simran made a note of it. Inside pages contained articles by political commentators as to why one party did fairly well and the other routed.

During her lecture in the college she was careful that she sounded unbiased. All was discussed. AIADMK and its cult culture, Samajwadi Party and its vote bank.

Simran sipped water. She had spoken continuously for the last forty - five minutes, as her students listened to her silently. Nothing gave her more pleasure than seeing her students listen to her intently as she taught, analyzed, and commented.

'Political Parties is an important topic, and you get a question on it every year.'

She could see a girl, sitting in the front row, mark the chapter in red. She wrote the statistics she had taken from the newspaper, with a yellow chalk, and tried to explain the performance of each political party.

She came back by two - thirty, exhausted. Sunita brought a chilled bottle of water.

'You need to get the gas booked,' Sunita spoke, her forehead furrowed, 'I have borrowed the cylinder from Praseetha Amma.' Praseetha Amma was an elderly lady who lived in the same building. She was all alone, and sought Sunita's help whenever required. Simran searched for her black diary in which she had noted down all the important telephone numbers.

'Hello, Meera Gas Agency,' a voice cackled.

Simran gave her consumer number and made a request for early delivery of the gas cylinder.

She had a light lunch and lay down. Sunita started rubbing her feet.

'We need to buy a television,' she was telling her mistress, her hands on her legs. 'When you are in the college, I get bored.'

Simran made a mental note of it. She wanted to withdraw some amount from the ATM in the evening. At times Simran too wanted to watch the television post dinner. Sunita slept with her in her room, on the floor.

Simran made a mental calculation. She took an estimate of the balance remaining in her account after she had bought the television. When she was with Varun, she never bothered. Things were different now. She got up at five in the evening, and drank a hot cup of tea. Sunita cleaned her beige sandals, and helped her arrange the *saree* pleats. She took a taxi and directed the driver to a good market where they sold electronic goods. Nearly two hours were thus spent, hopping from one shop to another. Finally she settled on a twenty-nine inch Samsung television. She quickly made the payment, counting the crisp bank notes twice over, and jotted down the address of the shop on a small sheet of paper.

'We will make the delivery tomorrow in the morning,' the salesman, a thin man with pencil moustaches, informed her.

Simran nodded.

Praseetha Amma came over on Sunday. She had gathered all the information about Simran from Sunita.

'Ask your son to visit you more frequently,' the large *bindi* shone on her head as she sat next to Simran, talking to her comfortingly. Sunita always showed her mistress in good light.

'Living alone is not easy,' she sighed, 'I have been doing it for the last ten years.'

'Your children?' Simran enquired hesitatingly.

'All settled abroad,' the old lady said, 'no one has time for an old woman.'

'I do not want to live with them,' she added, 'it is boring, sitting at home all alone, with nothing to do.'

Sunita entered the room, carrying a large tray. Simran offered sweets to Praseetha Amma.

'No, no, severe case of diabetes,' the old woman moved her large head to and fro, 'only tea, nothing else.'

'Sunita told me you were on the beach when the sea struck,' the old woman had finished her tea, and was in no hurry to leave.

Simran remained silent.

'Many died. I went to Marina Beach. The bodies stank, I vomited twice. But I donated Rupees ten thousand from my personal account.'

'My memsahib is a brave woman,' by now Sunita had settled comfortably, resting her back against the wall.

'Yes, of course', the old lady looked at Simran fondly.

'Amma,' Simran spoke finally, 'I want to buy some potted plants. Can you help me?'

'You don't need to worry,' the old lady said. 'Tomorrow, after you have gone to the college, I will go with Sunita and select the plants for you.'

The plants came in the evening. Simran placed the palm, with its curved, slender branches, in her living room. They had also bought some hanging pots for the terrace. She bought a couple of garden chairs, with a tiny centre table. Simran could now have her tea on the terrace. It reminded her of her young days, when she was newly married. Varun and she took pride in small things they bought.

She placed a few pots upside down, and some circular pots were placed above them. Small earthen pots were placed between the bars. The place looked nice enough, Sunita surveyed with some pride.

One day Simran took Sunita to Marina Beach. Sunita had never seen sea earlier. She looked with awe at the lashing waves, as Simran sat. Both her legs spread, she looked at the turbulent waters lazily. She sipped cold water from the flask, filled with ice cubes. Sunita placed both her feet in water, and splashed some on her face.

Simran came and sat beside Sunita quietly. 'Sunita, did your sahib ever miss me?'

'No,' Sunita replied.

'Who cooks for him now?'

'A part time maid who comes in the morning.'

'Can she prepare good *aloo paranthas*?'

Suddenly Simran had the urge to get into deep waters and be carried away by the waves.

Probably no one would miss her.

'Let us get back,' Simran sprang to her feet. She did not have her dinner. She had lost her appetite. A jilted lover and a rejected wife are not exactly the happiest.

'Those who can take their lives are gutsy,' Simran whispered.

'I would call them cowards,' Sunita shot back, 'only someone strong can take life, head on.'

'Switch off the light and bring your things close to my bed,' Simran instructed, her eyes wide open.

'Memsahib, you should have put your foot down.'

'One doesn't listen where matters of heart are concerned.'

'Have you ever loved anyone, memsahib?'

Simran thought of William. She remembered him, his tongue probing her, and his hands all over her body.

Did William love her? Or was it lust? If he were in love, he would have come for Simran. Maybe he just wanted some fun; he had it, now it did not matter.

But deep down, Simran knew William would come to her one day. She had the urge to go to Sothavilai. At least Mary could have rung up, she had her mobile number.

Sunita watched her mistress intently. Simran had been silent for a long time. Sunita had her answer. She thanked God silently. Let my mistress have some joy in life.

Bunny called up. Early in the morning, as usual. Simran rubbed her eyes and stretched her hand towards the table, where the mobile rang continuously. He was asking her to join him for his college festival.

The festival was after a fortnight. For the first time in her life, Simran went to the ticket counter, standing at the end of a queue. She sweated profusely, as she stood there, waiting for her turn. Men jostled with one another, the railway station was overcrowded.

A woman squatted on the ground, stretching one hand towards Simran, seeking alms. There was a stump where her right hand should have been, exposing the thick mat of hair on her armpit. Simran tossed a five rupee coin towards her. It fell a few feet away from her. The woman ran, she stumbled, and fell headlong, spilling the coins she had on the floor. The woman went mad. She waved threateningly at small, scantily clad children who ran to scoop the coins. Simran felt guilty. She left the queue and helped the woman retrieve her treasure. By the time she got her ticket, she was drained of all energy.

She stopped near a food counter and ordered a Mango Maaza. She inserted the pipe in the bottle, and took small sips. She saw an invalid woman inching close to her, her eyes fixed on her bottle. Simran ordered another bottle, and offered it to her. The woman brightened.

It was a Sunday. Praseetha Amma had invited them for lunch. She had got a telephone call from her son and she was happy. Normally the old lady had rice and curd for lunch but she had made elaborate preparations that day.

'Amma, how old are you?'

'Sixty-five.'

'What will you do when you are not able to take care of yourself?'

'I will kill myself. I will never be a dependent invalid.'

'My husband died when I was thirty and though my family offered help, I refused to accept it.'

Simran looked at the old lady admiringly. Here she was, with a nice job, a grown up son, and no liability!

And she was unhappy.

Praseetha Amma, a semi - educated woman, who did not know where her next meal came from, refused to accept support from family.

They sat in the balcony after the lunch. Some plants had wilted; the old lady did not have the energy to tend to them properly. Later Simran asked her maid to go to the old lady and help her out.

The three were happy together; Simran would forget about her problems at such times.

'I am preparing spicy pickles,' Praseetha Amma told Simran one day, 'take them for your son when you go to him.'

Bunny came to the railway station in trousers, with a lot of pockets, and a navy blue T-shirt with a round neck. He hugged his mother. The taxi screeched to a halt at the hotel portico. The bags were carried to a room, large in size, with a double bed. Simran was helped by her son in emptying the bags. The *sarees* were hung in the cupboard, the sandals unwrapped, and arranged in a row. The lipsticks were placed next to the hairbrush, on the dressing table. Everything seemed to be in order.

'Pickles for you,' Simran held out the small jar she had carried from Chennai. She placed it carefully in a poly bag and handed it over to her son.

'Does Papa send the money to you in time?'

'Yes. In fact, he has started sending something extra to me.'

'Go for a haircut.'

Bunny smiled.

Simran reached early, and got a seat in the front row. After the inauguration, there was a welcome dance. Girls stood in two rows, in heavy *saree* and jewellery, and gave a dazzling performance. A boy mimicked; the audience laughed.

It was time for Bunny's performance. He sat on a low chair, with a guitar in hand. Simran listened to her son perform. The audience clapped. It was late when the show was over.

She stayed with her son for two more days. She purchased him a watch.

'Don't overspend, you need money right now,' Bunny said quietly, 'Papa sends enough to me.'

'Your mother earns, and she can afford to gift a watch to her son.'

Bunny tweaked Simran's nose.

'When are you inviting me to your new house?'

'Come over during vacations.'

Bunny had come in shorts and T-shirt to see his mother off. He wore slippers, his hair was tousled.

'Did you drink yesterday?'

'No, Ma, I don't drink.' There was a glint in his eyes.

Simran patted him. 'Take care of yourself,' she shouted as Bunny ran, waving. The train pulled off.

She reached Chennai late in the evening. The porter ran to her. The suitcase was perched on his shoulders. Had she been in Delhi, Varun would have sent the driver. Here in Chennai, she stood all alone, her luggage at her feet, waiting for a taxi.

Simran felt lonely.

She reached home in ten minutes. Sunita opened the door. The television was on, and Praseetha Amma was sitting on the sofa, cross - legged, the coffee cup in her hand. Simran had requested her to stay with Sunita in her absence.

Sunita placed a fresh towel in the bathroom.

'Tell us about Bunny baba,' Sunita was very close to Bunny.

'Bunny is well. He misses you.'

'Is your son as tall as his father?' The old lady wanted to know more.

'Bunny baba is the tallest amongst his friends,' Sunita spoke fondly, while brushing her mistress' hair.

'Did he like my pickles?'

'He has asked me to send some more by parcel.'

The old lady beamed. She was confident none made pickles like her.

Sunita laid the table. An extra plate was laid for Praseetha Amma. The old woman slurped her curd and rice while Sunita ran around.

'Why didn't you go for another child?' the old lady had finished eating, and was now washing her hands.

'I didn't conceive.'

'Are you sure? Or did you take preventive measures?'

'Bringing up more than one would have been tough.'

'Children are never a source of burden,' the old lady shook her head, 'they are God's gift to us.'

Sunita wanted to know about Bunny's performance. 'He played well,' Simran remarked, 'though I had this temptation to pull his hair off his forehead.'

'He told me he was going to get his hair spiked, Beckham style.'

By now Sunita had stopped brushing Simran's hair; Simran rested her head on a pillow. Her wet hair spread out, snake-like.

'How did you spend your days?'

It was now Simran's turn to make enquiries.

'I hardly understand the language here,' Sunita lamented, 'the grocer talks to me in sign language.'

'When I ask him for sugar, he gives me pulses. When I ask for pulses, I get salt.'

Simran smiled. It must be an interesting situation. The grocer being harangued by her maidservant; and the maidservant banging her head on discovering what she had brought home, stomping back to the shop, shouting at the grocer.

One thing was certain. Simran would have had a tough time if these two women were not there.

Simran shut her eyes. She was tired. The day was long and strenuous and she had to go to the college the following day. Praseetha Amma was staying back with them. The voices became less and less audible as Simran fell asleep. Sunita checked the main gate, shut it, and then switched off the lights.

The two women had risen much before Simran did. The old woman was muttering something religious while taking bath. Sunita was busy in the kitchen, preparing breakfast. She banged the bathroom door.

'Amma, you must hurry up.'

Praseetha Amma emerged, chanting something. The clothes she had washed were in her hands.

The old woman had breakfast with Simran.

Simran dressed up, wearing a green and yellow *saree*, with mirror work.

As she took short, swift strides towards her college, Simran thought of Mary. Simran was often told, Delhi was heartless, selfish. Mary was not a Delhiite, and she was heartless. Whenever Simran went to the beach, she remembered Mary. Once Mary had pulled her deep into water, and she laughed aloud as Simran spluttered, her eyes, nose and ears filled with water. Mary was lively, the zeal of living was plainly reflected in her eyes.

Simran had reached her college gate. Some of her students greeted her. She nodded. She reached her classroom, pulled a chair, and sat down. Her feet were slightly swollen. Though Sunita insisted she put her feet in salt and water, the swelling did not subside. Simran sat and taught.

'Ma'am, you are wearing a lovely *saree*,' one of her students, sitting in the third row, complimented her. Simran smiled.

'Where did you buy it from?'

'Delhi.'

'Ma'am, why did you come all the way to Chennai?'

'Chennai fascinates me.'

The student was not convinced.

Simran had difficulty in walking. All of a sudden she slipped, falling into a small ditch. She felt shooting pain as a passer-by ran to help her. She was lifted with some difficulty. A young boy collected Simran's purse and books, and handed them over to her. By the time she reached home, her left foot was so swollen it hardly fitted into her slipper. She removed the slippers, and walked, barefooted.

Simran slumped on a chair. She relaxed, as Sunita fussed around.

Praseetha Amma pressed at the injured spot. Simran cried out.

'I think you have fractured your foot,' she surmised.

'No, no, it is just a swelling. It will subside.'

When the swelling did not subside for two - three days, they took Simran to an orthopaedic.

'But doctor, it cannot be a fracture. It does not hurt much.'

The doctor pressed the affected area, and Simran groaned.

'So now you know,' he smiled.

Simran had gone to the orthopaedic in a blue dress. They took a sharp blade and cut the dress right up to the knee.

'You are wearing a blue dress. Do you want your plaster in blue?'

Simran thought for a while, and then said, yes.

They put her in a wheel chair. A taxi was called. She was wheeled in.

She was held by Sunita and Praseetha Amma. The doctor had advised she should restrict her movement for the first twenty-four hours. Simran looked at the plaster with disgust.

She decided to catch on with her reading.

'Don't read in dim light,' Praseetha Amma had scolded her as she saw Simran, her foot on the stool, and her eyes glued to the book.

'Such tiny prints,' she sat nearby, examining the novel, and its cover. Simran shut the book.

'Amma, tell me something about your late husband.'

'What do I tell you?' Simran could see a tinge of red on the old woman's cheeks.

'He was in government service and did not earn much. But every time he went on tour, he bought small gifts for me.'

'At times it was a pair of glass bangles, or may be a blouse piece,' the old woman continued.

'He always remembered my birthday. A few days before he died, he had gone to the jeweller, and ordered a beautiful gold chain for me.' The old lady's face glowed. She had fond memories of her husband.

'And then he died, leaving me alone.'

'What about your children? Did they miss their father?'

'They were very young when he died. Both of them.' Praseetha Amma was straining her memory. 'I don't think they remembered him much.'

'I became the man of the family,' the old woman went on. 'Leaving my children with my mother-in-law, I started working with an NGO. We made embroidered bed sheets, table clothes, mats, and sent them for sale in the market.'

'My mother-in-law died. Her back was bent with age. But by then, my children had grown up,' the old woman concluded dismissively.

Varun called up.

'Bunny told me you went to attend his college festival,' he shouted. 'Why didn't you tell me? We would have gone together.'

There was silence in the room. The old woman was straining her ears.

'My husband,' Simran whispered.

'I intend to buy another piece of property. Do you want me to buy a house for you in Chennai?'

'No,' Simran replied after a few seconds. 'Buy something for Bunny.'

'O.K. But where?'

'Ask him where he would like to set up his practice.'

'Do you intend to stay in Chennai for sometime?' Varun was probing.

'It depends.'

'Shall I send you some money? Bunny tells me you haven't bought a refrigerator yet.'

'I will buy it with this month's salary.' Simran was defensive.

'How much should I send?'

'Nothing.' Simran was firm. Her face had turned crimson.

Varun got the hint.

'Think it over. I will ring up after two days.'

Simran saw Praseetha Amma leaving; she was telling Sunita something in her ears. Sunita nodded, looking at Simran with sympathy.

It took almost a month for the foot to heal. Simran was taken to the doctor. He cut the plaster.

Simran walked funnily for a few days. Her legs had become stiff. She straightened a leg and walked.

Bunny had come for a day. He snuggled close to Simran, and laughed at the colour of her plaster.

'Such a bright blue,' he had laughed, 'what made you opt for this colour?'

'I was wearing a dress of the same colour.'

'When I break my bones, I will go to the doctor wearing a red shirt.'

Simran laughed.

'What will you have for dinner, baba?' Sunita stood at the doorway, looking at Bunny fondly.

'Delicious *chhole bhature* which only Sunita can prepare.'

When Bunny was leaving, Sunita packed *chhole* and few *bhature* in a large case. Bunny hugged Simran, and gave a peck on Sunita's cheeks.

Both the women waved as the taxi pulled off.

Summer was approaching. A cool breeze blew.

The big bamboo pole on the road swayed.

Simran went to the beauty parlour.

'Rupees six hundred,' the beautician said in a business-like manner, when Simran was through. Simran unzipped her purse, pulling out two five hundred rupee notes. The balance was handed over to her.

Simran felt nice. She always felt young and beautiful after every such session. She started humming a romantic tune, thinking of William and her stay with his family.

'Tomorrow I will ring up Mary,' she took a resolution, searching for her number.

13

He Sleeps Badly

It was late at night when Varun came back. Swati was with him. She was feeling sleepy. She carried a tiny earthen pot, with a few shoots of Rajnigandha plant. She took the pot to the bedroom and placed it carefully on the windowsill.

'The flower will keep the room fragrant,' she smiled as she followed Varun to the bathroom. Together they took a quick shower.

They dressed up hurriedly and drove towards the lake, five kilometers away. It was surrounded by thick trees, and overgrown vegetation. They wandered, walking very close. There was eerie silence.

They lay under a tree, the branches drooped down. He held Swati with his hands tightly. He bent over her and started licking her. She cried with sheer pleasure, clawing him, and holding on to him.

The leaves rustled as the two bodies moved.

They were late for the court the next morning. Varun sat in his chamber. Swati had gone to take an adjournment. He thought of his wife.

Varun had seen a distinct change in Simran over the last few years. She had mellowed, and took less interest in what he did.

For more than three years, he was with Swati. He was waiting for Simran to react as a typical jealous wife would, scratch his face as rumours of his infidelity reached her. Simran did no such thing. Neither did she skip her meals. She was silent, as if she knew nothing.

Varun was certain Sunita had told Simran all about him and Swati. He was expecting her to come down to Delhi, stomping, creating a scene. Simran did not come. He expected she would come during Christmas vacations and tell him that she was staying back, that she had abandoned her course.

But Simran was communicating less and less. Earlier she shared almost everything with him, the smallest detail. Now she did not communicate with him at all.

When his wife wanted to go to Chennai, he had been happy. He wanted his freedom, he had it. He spent all his time with Swati.

But Varun missed Simran too. He had loved her, and was devoted to her once. The two had brought up Bunny together, experiencing the pain and pleasure of parenthood. Every small thing bore Simran's imprint. The sheet on which he slept with Swati, the chairs on which they sat.

Varun had concentrated on his profession, he did not have time to look to family affairs. Simran took care of home. Teaching is not very taxing and she had time for her family. Simran had loved her home and took pains to make it beautiful.

Varun was attracted towards Swati right from the beginning. She stimulated him physically and intellectually. When Varun discussed a case with Swati, he experienced pure bliss. But what would Bunny think? Varun loved his son and did not want to lose respect in his eyes.

One morning, Varun rang her up. Simran was in the bathroom. Sunita took the call.

'Sahib, we have a television now,' Sunita was bubbling. 'When memsahib gets her next salary, we will buy a refrigerator.'

Varun felt bad.

'How big is the house, Sunita?'

'It is small, but we manage.'

Varun had decided. He was going to talk to some local property dealer and purchase a house for Simran.

'No', Simran was firm.

'You can buy something for Bunny,' she had suggested.

Was Simran showing her resentment?

At times Varun resolved he would have nothing to do with Swati. The moment he saw her face, his resolve disappeared. In the beginning, Varun's intention was to have some fun; but before he could realize, he was in love with her. It was a different ball game altogether.

'I have never been so happy,' Varun had told Swati once.

He was cheerful; everything appeared bright. Separation from Swati was unbearable. If Swati went away for a week, life was miserable. He waited for her call every minute; if he did not talk to her for a day, he was restless. His life centred around Swati.

When Swati informed Varun, 'My parents are searching for a suitable boy to marry me off,' he had gone mad.

He felt he still loved Simran and did not want to see her in pain. At the same time, he could not get over Swati. She had entered his system.

He wanted to do all he could to make Simran comfortable.

The proposal to buy the house was the first step. But Simran had refused. Varun's heart ached when he thought of Simran living without basic comforts.

'Let me send you a cheque. You can buy an AC and a refrigerator.'

'I can live without AC and I will buy the refrigerator after I get my salary next month.'

Sunita felt bad when she overheard their conversation.

'What is wrong with taking money from your husband?' she had muttered, her brows knitted.

Simran picked up her purse and left for the college.

Varun talked to Bunny in the evening, when his classes were over.

'Convince your mother to take a cheque from me.'

'I was going to talk to you about that, Papa,' Bunny replied. 'I have seen Ma live in near penury when I went to Chennai during vacations.'

'I want to buy a house for her but she wants me to do something for you instead.'

'Papa,' Bunny was speaking rapidly, 'we must do something for Ma.'

Varun hung up. He had a vague feeling his son knew what was going on. Bunny was an adult. Varun fervently hoped his son would not blame him.

He consulted Swati.

She was of no help.

Varun proposed to buy the house in the joint names of Simran and Bunny. Simran relented.

Varun said he was coming to Chennai by next week. A deal was struck.

It was a double - storeyed house, with a tiny lawn in front. A wrought iron swing was hung in the lawn. There were four bedrooms, large in size.

'Shall I buy you a car?'

'My college is nearby. I will walk down.'

'And if you have to go elsewhere?'

'I take a taxi.'

Varun returned after ten days. Swati was at the airport to receive him. They drove down to the court. The corridor was filled with lawyers. As Varun walked down, a middle-aged lawyer swished past him, his gown swaying as he ran.

Varun stopped near the electronic board, and took an assessment of the matters. He had four. He had to argue two himself, and in the other two, he had instructed senior counsel. Swati and Atishi were asked to be with the seniors in case he was stuck up in his other two matters.

Suman had gone to the registry to file a case. He came back hurriedly. He had to keep an eye on the board. He had to be present in each courtroom when the matter was argued. Bringing the brief to the courtroom, and keeping it back in the bag was his duty. He also ran to search for the senior counsel. The latter was on his legs in some other court.

At the end of the day the entire team came back, exhausted. They drove down to the office, where they sat and distributed work for the next day's appearance in court. Occasionally Varun passed on small cases to his juniors, and no one was surprised when Swati got the best matters.

Atishi and Suman smiled as Varun ran upstairs with Swati. Varun's office was on first floor.

'With ma'am not around, Sir is having a good time,' Atishi smiled, as he helped Suman take the bags out of the car.

Varun went for a shower. Swati selected his dress. Savitri, the new maid, was taking a nap. Swati woke her up and asked her to make tea.

Varun emerged from the bathroom, with a towel wrapped around his body. He wore blue jeans and black T-shirt. Varun wore perfume and sat beside Swati; the latter was leafing through a magazine. Savitri brought tea in two large mugs.

She went downstairs with tea for Atishi and Suman.

'Where is Swati?' Atishi asked.

'She is with sahib.'

Varun came downstairs, with Swati. He sat in his chamber, and called for the steno typist. Suman had seen the cause list and had marked the next day's matters. Varun stopped midway, as Atishi entered his room.

'Sir, I have to go now,' he said hesitatingly, 'which matter shall I do tomorrow?'

At the top of the cause list, Suman had written the names of the cases, along with the court and item numbers. Varun thought for a few seconds.

'Ask Suman to give you the brief,' he said, putting his finger on the third case in the list.

'Read it carefully', Varun smiled, 'there is no senior in this case. You have to argue it.'

Atishi left, his brief in his hands. Suman also left around 9 p.m. Swati called up her mother.

'Ma, I am going to Bombay for a matter by tonight's flight. I will come back day after.'

Swati's mother was worried. She had been happy with her daughter's success. But she sensed something was wrong. Whenever she broached the topic of marriage, Swati grew impatient.

'Where are you staying in Bombay?' Swati's mother enquired.

'I don't know. I will have to ask Varun sir.'

'Is it essential to go on tours?'

'Yes mamma. Professionally I will do well only if I go to other courts too.'

Swati hung up hurriedly.

'So, mamma is not convinced,' Varun yawned, and switched on the T.V.

'Varun, at times I feel terribly scared.'

Varun ruffled Swati's hair. He got up to make drinks. With Savitri going home tonight, things had become easier. Swati stayed back.

They drank together, drinking from the same glass. Varun motioned towards Swati to come closer. He caressed her. They drank for an hour after which Swati heated food and brought it to the bedroom. Varun helped Swati remove the utensils to the kitchen.

'Savitri will never get suspicious that you were here.'

'I have bought a nice house for Simran in Chennai. I saw to furnishings too.'

'What next?'

'I intend to buy a car for her.'

'Good.'

Both watched a movie. None spoke for the next half an hour.

'Varun I have got a nice offer from an IIM graduate. He likes me and my family,' Swati spoke finally, not looking at Varun. 'There is a lot of pressure from my family to marry him.'

Varun continued watching television, lowering its volume.

He slept badly that night. The thought of Swati leaving terrified him.

14

Treachery

The sky was muddy, totally black. Simran felt a surge of pleasure as darkness enveloped her. It would rain, she was certain.

'Sunita, do not wash the clothes today,' she shouted, as she ran down the stairs.

Simran recalled the way river Yamuna swelled during the monsoon. Otherwise, it was a mere drain most of the year. She loved peeping down, holding the railing of the bridge as wind swept, and tiny drops of water fell on her face. Once, when she drove down the DND flyway, she stopped the car. She got down and stayed there for half an hour.

She was in mood today. It had started raining; drops of water danced, and made small pools. She felt like spreading her arms and dance as droplets fell on her hair, her cheeks. Her clothes stuck to her.

She came back, drenched. Sunita got her fresh clothes and ginger flavoured tea.

'Get me hot *pakodas,*' she asked, as Sunita set down the teacup before her mistress. Sunita was busy in the kitchen, preparing the batter, cutting thin strips of onion and green chillies. She had switched on the music; they played songs on rain on FM, the radio channel.

It rained hard, water creeping in. Sunita got a wiper from the bathroom, and wiped the floor.

Rain hammered on the asbestos sheets above. Simran called up Mary. A sleepy voice responded, hardly recognizable.

'Hi Mary,' she chirped, 'remember your old roommate?'

'Oh Simran! Where are you dear?'

'Right here, in Chennai.'

'What? Don't tell me! Didn't you go back to Delhi?'

'No. I have got a transfer to Chennai.'

'I don't believe this!' the young woman now sounded more familiar, her voice was bubbly.

'We have been living in the same town, and we have not met!'

'So, when are you coming over?'

'Today itself, in the evening.'

They sat in Simran's garden. Mary was impressed, as she took a round of Simran's house. She sat on her bed, and spread her legs, taking a pillow on her lap.

'Now tell me all about yourself,' she was relaxed, and wanted to know more about the older woman.

'I don't have much to say,' Simran smiled, 'I think you need to tell me about yourself.'

Mary smiled, as she saw Simran staring at her.

'Yes, I have got married. What else?'

'You talk of your marriage as if you have got a tooth extracted.'

Mary guffawed.

'Well, I have married the same man who came on motorcycle every day. His mother stays with us and gives me a tough time.'

Simran made a face.

'You will never change.'

'And if it is of interest to you, I am pregnant.'

'How many months?'

'Four.'

'Do you take Autrin, Folvite–all these medicines regularly?'

'Yes. Don't worry. I don't walk up and down the stairs a lot. I take fruits, green vegetables, milk, everything. Anything more?'

'Fine.'

'Good. Now shall we go out in your garden and get soaked?'

'O.K.'

Both women made a spectacle of themselves, holding hands like two small children, as water splashed on their faces.

Sunita looked down from the window; she smiled fondly as she saw one run as the other walked. Simran's face glowed as she sat with Mary, completely soaked. Simran talked about Bunny and his studies. She sounded happy when she discussed her son.

'Didn't your husband insist that you go back?' Mary was curious.

'He has a young woman.'

Mary looked at Simran with large, sympathetic eyes. She had always felt that Simran was one who had it all–looks, money, happiness. And she had often wondered why she left her home and came to Chennai. As she looked at the older woman, she felt a tenderness towards her.

She embraced Simran.

Simran composed herself.

'Well Mary, take care of yourself. Do not lift heavy things.'

Mary understood Simran wanted to change the topic.

'Do you go for regular checkups?'

'Yes. Every month. It is interesting sitting with others with bloated bellies, waiting for the doctor.'

'Is your husband happy?'

'I haven't seen him happier.'

'When do I get to meet your husband?'

'Come for lunch this Sunday.'

Simran agreed.

'You don't exert yourself. I will cook and get something from home.'

Praseetha Amma was at home, with Sunita, when Simran went over to Mary's place. Mary was standing near the entrance, one of her elbows resting on the gate. She smiled as she saw Simran get down from the taxi, and walked down to meet her.

'Nice to meet you as Mary's husband,' Simran smiled, as she saw the man she had seen often.

They had a small and neat accommodation. Mary had done up the house tastefully. Small lampshades, made of bamboo, were hung at the corners of the living room. There were mattresses at both the ends, and cushions casually thrown all over. There was a tiny centre table, with four chairs around it. Huge hangings, with semi-nude women, adorned the walls.

They talked of their stay together. Simran was careful not to talk of unpleasant things. She caught Mary staring at her, searching for something in her eyes. When Simran looked at her, she simply smiled, and looked away.

'How is everyone at home?'

'Mamma is alright. Matilda is yet to get over the shock.'

Simran could not muster courage to ask her about William. Neither did Mary tell her about him. Sothavilai was something she would rather not talk about.

Mary's husband was jovial. He talked a lot, and cracked jokes. Simran was amused to see the manner in which he talked of Mary, Sothavilai. He had something funny to say about each member of her family.

'And her brother William,' he went on, 'when I have talked to him for half an hour, I get a one-sentence reply.'

Simran laughed.

'Matilda walks like a sailing ship.'

'I am sure you will have something to say about me too once I am gone.'

He guffawed.

'Enough,' Mary arched her eyebrows, 'if you continue making fun of my family and friends, I will walk out of this house this instant. Now that I have Simran, I will not worry about alternative accommodation.' Her eyes twinkled as she spoke.

'Oh no, please don't,' Mary's husband showed mock fear. 'I can't live without you.' He was immediately at her feet.

'Stop being dramatic,' Mary smiled, pushing off her husband who had now caught her legs.

'Simran, why did I marry him?'

'Because dear, no one else would have married you.'

'Uh-h-h, I had six marriage proposals, all good ones.'

'Stop fighting,' Simran intervened. 'I am famished. Shall we eat something?'

The couple got up immediately and served the meal. After lunch, Simran and Mary went back to the living room. Mary's husband went out, to get ice cream.

'Life was miserable, Simran,' Mary was telling her. 'This man has made me laugh again.'

'Does Matilda know she cannot conceive?'

'Yes, and she is devastated.'

'Why do these things happen to us Simran?'

'It happens to all of us. You are hit when you least expect it.'

When Simran came back, she saw Sunita oiling Praseetha Amma's hair.

Simran sat on a low chair and started correcting the tutorial papers.

'Very busy?' Praseetha Amma was peering at her.

'I am through,' saying so, Simran shut her books, and started arranging the newspapers that were strewn around.

'How do you know Mary?'

'We were together for a short course.'

'I am not feeling well. I think I will stay back with you tonight.'

'You are welcome. You can sleep with me.'

Praseetha Amma did not sleep the entire night.

'Amma, stay with us. You are not in a position to go anywhere,' Simran said as she left for her college.

Simran took the classes. She handed over the tutorial papers to her students and then took a test. The test lasted two hours. Simran stood behind a student as she saw her scribbling her answers.

'What an atrocious handwriting,' she remarked. 'Your table is shaking vigorously. How do you manage to write?'

'Ma'am, I want to get it replaced.'

Simran summoned the peon.

'Go, get another table for her.'

Two peons entered the classroom, holding a new table.

After two hours, Simran collected the answer sheets. She stacked them together, put them in her purse, and left the classroom.

When Simran returned, she saw a huge crowd gather near her house. Maybe there was an accident, she was curious. She saw an old woman wail as half burnt bodies of a young woman and a child were being loaded on an ambulance. A small crowd had gathered. The old woman cried inconsolably.

'He has killed my daughter. What had she done to deserve this? He has not even spared the child! Why did I marry my daughter to this savage?'

Others were talking in whispers.

'He is an animal; he beat his wife regularly. He drank and returned, abusing his wife. An unlucky woman!'

Simran peered at the child. She was barely seven-eight, and looked elf-like, with her singed hair. Simran's heart filled with remorse as she saw the ambulance move, carrying the two to the hospital. She rang her doorbell. Sunita was keen to talk to Simran about the incident.

'I know the woman,' she was talking impatiently, 'we met regularly at the vegetable vendor's; the child was always with her, helping the mother carry the bag of vegetables.'

'I always sensed something was wrong with them. The child always looked frightened, and the mother spoke very little.'

'Why does one marry, memsahib?'

Simran threw a sidelong glance at her maid. Was she making an oblique reference to Simran and her marital life?

Simran hurried towards her bedroom. She threw her *saree* on the bed and wore a nightie. It was lacy, with no sleeves. Its neckline plunged low. She had her lunch on a tray. After lunch, Simran stretched on the bed. She dozed off.

When she got up, it was dark. She sat on the terrace, looking at the sky. Two men were busy cutting grass in the park. They had removed their shirts and moved with the grass cutting machine, in their vests. Their shirts were thrown on the bench.

Simran's thoughts went back to the half-burnt woman and her child. She thought again and again of the child, with singed hair. The bells she had hung in the terrace swung to and fro, like a pendulum. They were fastened to the iron bars with wires. Simran removed the dried leaves. She admired the plant she had hung near the bells. It had a sharp end and a white border. Another one, planted in a circular pot, stood erect, its leaves shuddering as wind blew. The men in the park had stopped working. With the machine switched off, it was quieter. They wore their shirts and sat on the bench, talking for a while. After a few minutes they got up, sat on their bicycles, and pedalled away.

Simran hoped they would come back the next day, completing the work. She wore her sports shoes and went for a walk. There were overgrown weeds all around; flower bushes were in a corner, with blooming, pink flowers. She went to the green belt, ten minutes walk from her house, and took a round. There were small benches. She walked briskly for half an hour. She sat on a bench, rested for ten minutes and then got up hurriedly.

Her mobile rang.

'Ma'am, I am one of your students. I need some help. Can I come over to your place today?'

'Certainly. Come around eight.'

Simran looked at her watch and hurried off.

The student had come with a pile of notebooks and question papers. Simran sat, marking out important questions, correcting the pile of notes. She decided to call it a day around eleven.

'Come tomorrow,' she instructed.

'At what time?'

'Around six in the evening.'

'Thanks ma'am,' saying so, the student left.

Sunita woke up Simran early the next day. It was drizzling. She threw an angry look at Sunita. Why did she have to wake me up so early on a Sunday?

'The child is dead,' Sunita whispered, 'they are bringing the dead body home.'

By now Simran was fully awake. She peeped out of the window. It was cool outside. It had rained the whole night. The body of the child was placed on the verandah. The old lady she saw yesterday sat next to the dead body.

Simran went and sat there, with other neighbours. The child's mother was battling for her life in the hospital. The old lady was the child's maternal grandmother.

'I will go to the highest court of the land,' the old woman snivelled, 'I will see to it that the man is hanged.'

'Leave it,' someone said softly, patting her.

'How can I? I have lost my granddaughter. Most probably my daughter too will die.'

'God will punish the guilty.'

More people started coming in. Simran got up, wore her slippers, and left.

The student came in the evening. He carried a box of sweets. They sat in the living room, spreading the notes on the table. Simran sat correcting the notes quietly. The student looked at her, peering whenever he saw Simran put a red mark and write comments.

'Your answers are average,' she said finally. She gave the names of some books.

'Consult these reference books and supplement your answers with them.'

The student left.

Simran stretched on the chair, putting both her legs on the table.

Sunita had switched on the television. She sat watching the soap, shedding tears. Simran smiled.

Simran wanted to have a glass of water. She poured water from a chilled bottle in the refrigerator.

'The refrigerator is dirty. Clean it tomorrow,' she instructed, wondering if Sunita heard her. She wondered if her maid was hard of hearing. She covered her ears with both her hands as she entered her bedroom, where Sunita sat on the floor, watching the programme.

'Lay the table when it is over.'

Sunita nodded, shedding more tears.

Probably Varun did not need Simran any longer.

It was all so paradoxical. Simran, who detested Varun for having an affair with his junior, was now doing what he had done. She loved William and looked forward to meeting him.

Varun always rang up Bunny to ask him about his mother. They were together for a long time, it could not be put away that easily.

'Food is laid,' Sunita nudged at her, wiping her tears.

She ate her dinner silently. If William loved her, why did he not contact her? And if Varun loved Swati, why was he so concerned about her?

Sunita talked about the dead child, as she ate.

A black Santro pulled up before the house adjacent to Simran's. A man emerged, wearing bottle green T-shirt and beige trousers.

'He comes here every night to meet the lady who lives on the first floor.'

'You seem to know the entire neighbourhood,' Simran remarked, craning her neck to catch a glimpse of the man's face.

It was William.

Simran ran to the window to confirm what she had seen.

Yes, it was he.

'The woman is a divorcee and lives alone with her children,' Sunita's voice rang in her ears.

She saw a petite lady open the door. A girl clutched at her, as she shut the door.

Simran was numb. She could not believe what she had seen. Sunita continued speaking, oblivious of what was hurting her mistress' mind.

She went to the bathroom and stood under the shower. She felt cool. She wanted to shut out all the thoughts from her mind.

She came to her bedroom, and removed the bedcover. Sunita was making her bed. She could not understand why her mistress had become so quiet.

'Switch off the light and go to sleep.'

Sunita obeyed her mistress.

Simran was restless. She got up stealthily, ensuring she did not wake up Sunita. She hit a table as she groped for her way. She pulled a chair and placed it near the window.

The black Santro stood there. It was past midnight. Children seemed to be asleep. It was quiet outside. Simran had the urge to run to the house where William had gone, and bang the door. She wanted to confront William and ask him questions.

But what would she ask?

Simran sat on the chair the whole night, looking out of her window. At five in the morning, she saw William emerge. He sat in his Santro and drove away.

Sunita stood behind Simran. She looked at William, and then at her mistress. Simran rubbed her eyes. She stretched herself on the chair.

'Get me a cup of tea,' she smiled at Sunita feebly.

'Memsahib, this lady has shifted here about fifteen days ago. She lived abroad, and has come here with her children after her divorce.'

'How many children does she have?' Simran was in a trance.

'Three, aged between five to eleven years.'

'Does that man come here every night?'

'Yes, every night.'

'How do you know?'

'Everyone knows. The entire neighbourhood talks about them.'

'Her children speak funnily. And everyone wants to talk to them.'

They must be speaking in accented English, Simran thought weakly.

She rang up Varun. Suddenly she missed him terribly.

'Yes,' he was half asleep.

'I thought I should thank you for the house and everything.'

Varun was surprised. What had happened to his wife? Why did she call up so early in the morning?

'What happened? Any problem?' he sounded concerned.

Simran remained irritable the whole day. In the evening she hired a cab and went to Marina Beach. She walked on sand, her feet digging in. A child made a sand castle. A young lad trod on it. The castle was flattened. The child's face contorted.

Simran continued walking; a man selling coconut water came to her.

She sat down, sipping coconut water, small grains of sand sticking to her. The sea howled; she felt soothed.

'Take this toy for your child,' a vendor selling a small drum, with sticks which had circular ends, came nearer. She thought of something and bought the toy. She decided to get it packed and send it to her new neighbour, for her children.

She looked at her toenails. They were overgrown, and hurt when she wore shoes. She thought of people who had perished when the tsunami had struck.

Simran's mind was in turmoil. She wanted to meet William when he came in the evening. She wanted to stand right where he parked his car; he could not ignore her.

Her heart beat fast. She had to take a decision. She could not bear the agony any longer. From the beach she would go straight to where she had seen William yesterday, lurking in dark, waiting for him. She had one more coconut water. She held on to the coconut, like an oblong breast, with both her hands. She took small sips. She needed to kill three to four hours. An old woman sat near her, looking at her reassuringly. Simran smiled at her.

'Do you come here often?' the woman struck a conversation.

'May be once or twice a week,' Simran replied.

'What about you?'

'I come here every day. It is a relief to sit here after a hard day's work.'

'What do you do, Amma?' Simran was happy she could distract her mind from William.

'I have a small grocery shop where I keep all the essential items. My days are very busy.'

'Do you manage the shop alone?'

'No, my grandchild helps me.'

The old lady dusted herself, and got up.

'It is quite late,' she flashed a toothless smile, and waved at her.

Simran walked back, slowly. She had an hour to reach her destination. A taxi pulled before her.

She stood in a corner, at a distance of ten paces from where William parked his car. It was nine thirty. William's car did not appear. She waited till ten thirty. Sunita had said he came there every day. She waited there for an hour. He did not come.

At eleven she saw the lady, whom William came to meet, put a big lock on the front gate and switch off the lights. The children were taken in, and all the lights were switched off. It was quiet all around. Simran had an impulse to talk to the lady. She changed her mind. What would she tell her? That she was interested in her man?

She flung her clothes in the bathroom and went to bed. Sunita had been standing near the window when Simran waited for William. She had recognized her mistress.

She asked no questions.

15

She Leaves

'Varun, what to do? Should I refuse to marry that IIM graduate?' Swati looked at Varun, her eyes fixed on him.

Varun remained silent.

Swati waited for a minute. She asked again, gently, 'Does our relationship have any future?'

'No,' Varun gave a crisp reply.

'I want to turn down the marriage proposal. I have given enough hints to my mother.'

'Don't,' Varun was serious.

'Don't refuse the proposal,' he added.

Swati was shocked. Was he the same Varun who said life had become beautiful after she had come into his life? Varun always said he felt restless if he did not meet Swati for a day.

'Yes, of course,' Swati said, her face a picture of sorrow. Today she found a different Varun.

'Well then I take leave,' Swati spoke abruptly, getting up.

'Sit for two more minutes,' Varun caught her hand and forced her to sit down. He was scribbling on his notepad feverishly. He looked tense.

'I need to go,' Swati's voice was cold.

'I will walk down with you,' Varun spoke, still in tension.

Both walked in silence.

'I will feel guilty accepting someone as my husband after the kind of relationship we have had.'

'Don't be stupid,' Varun's voice was cold. 'You should have felt guilty earlier, having an affair with a married man.'

Swati had had enough.

'O.K., I am going,' she quickened her pace.

'Wait for a while', Varun was visibly tense. 'I am ready to help in any manner I can.'

'I don't want your help,' Swati shot back. What kind of help was he offering? Money?

Swati felt disgusted.

She left.

Swati's mother looked at her daughter stand on the doorway, pressing the doorbell continuously. She looked surprised, as she stepped aside, making way for Swati.

'Eat something,' she entered Swati's room. She knew something was hurting her daughter, and she was wise enough not to ask questions.

'I have a severe headache, Ma. I can't eat anything.' Swati's mother put the plate aside, and sat beside her daughter. She pressed her head gently.

Swati felt exhausted; her eyelids drooped as her mother's gentle fingers massaged her; switching off the light, Swati's mother left the room gently.

Swati got up at two in the morning. Her bedroom was flooded with moonlight. Everything came back to her mind. What had she done? Her life was in complete shambles. She had always been impetuous; she took the plunge and thought about it later. For the first time in life she felt insecure. I am feeling miserable right now, she was telling herself. Maybe one month from now, the pain would not be so intense. Let me read something, she decided. She switched on the light, picked up a book, and started reading. She could not concentrate. She thought of the previous day.

'I had your consent all along,' Varun had said.

Swati nodded. She had always consented.

She started thinking of Varun. He had always been scared of his wife, Swati suspected. He was very particular that his wife knew nothing. He had behaved boldly, making the relationship intense only after his wife had left for Chennai. And at times, Swati felt, Varun trivialized her in front of his wife so that she did not suspect anything.

Swati was also to be blamed for her situation. If she wanted, she could have put a stop to everything right in the beginning. But she had done no such thing. She had liked Varun. She had paid for it. Her heart ached every time she thought of Varun.

Varun called up the next day. 'I hope you are fine.'

'Yes.'

'I miss you.'

She hung up.

She went to the park and sat on an iron bench. Two old men, around seventy, sat there, looking at her. Swati ignored them. Her thoughts were elsewhere.

Swati was twenty - three while Varun was forty - five, a huge age gap. And Varun had helped her in the profession. She could not understand why she had been so hurt when she heard of Varun's response. Maybe Varun could have been more gentle. She did not want Varun to say what she had known all along. And he had said it harshly.

Teenage love is immature, and less calculating. One talks of stars and moon and cries when one realizes that these cannot be reached.

Swati knew Varun loved his wife. He always defended her. She could sense his nervousness when his wife gave a call on his mobile. Twenty years of marriage was a long association. But she had seen few husbands who were as scared of their wives as Varun.

Swati wondered why she had got herself into such a mess. Anyway, a decision had to be taken.

She talked to her mother.

'I am ready to marry,' she said, with composure.

And she was married within a month.

16

The Marriage

Swati was the youngest of the three sisters. Both her sisters worked hard towards preparations for Swati's marriage. They shopped all day, leaving their children to their mother's care. Swati's father was an electrical engineer with GAIL. He was about to retire, and he made every effort to make her wedding memorable.

Swati would generally spend her time in her room, pretending she was preparing for her cases. But most of the time she was lost in thoughts, recalling the moments she had spent with Varun. She felt terribly scared. Young men and women were more open about sex during present times, and pre-marital sex was no longer a taboo. But she was apprehensive. She wondered how her husband would react when he would come to know.

Love is a beautiful feeling; but the accompanying sense of guilt takes away half the fun.

Swati's sisters were beautiful, demure, and had been married for some years. They cooked and cleaned, brought up children and led fulfilled lives. Their husbands drew a decent salary, and took care of their needs.

Swati was different. She was bright, and had been very ambitious, right from the beginning. At times she felt her ambition was her bane. Had she been unambitious like her sisters, she would have led a contented life.

A young niece came panting to her room, carrying a bundle of *sarees*.

'Look at these,' she spoke rapidly, 'these are for you. Ma said I should show them to you and bring them back.' Saying so, the little girl sat on a small chair, dropping the bundle on Swati's bed.

'Tomorrow you may have to accompany Ma to the market,' the child spoke, 'to get your blouses tailored.'

Swati smiled. She put the *sarees* in the child's hands, kissed her, and asked her to take them back carefully.

Swati met Varun near the tailor's shop. He removed his sunglasses, and looked at Swati, a puzzled look on his face.

'My senior,' she introduced him to her sisters. Her sisters greeted him, folding their hands.

'Wedding preparations?'

Swati gave him a weak smile. Then he went away.

'Your senior is a handsome man,' a sister said.

They reached their tailor. They gave all the blouse pieces to him for stitching.

'Swati, tell me honestly, was there something between you and your senior?' a sister blurted out.

Swati gave a startled look to her sister. Who had told her all this?

She shrugged, and left the shop. She remained silent as they drove back.

'Do you want to have an ice cream?' her sisters looked concerned.

'No,' she gave a crisp reply.

'Come downstairs, the dinner is ready,' her mother stood near the staircase, and called.

'I don't want to eat,' Swati said.

Her mother climbed upstairs. She saw Swati, curled up on her chair, looking vacantly.

'I have got your food for you,' the mother sat near her daughter, and nudged at her gently.

'Ma, please go', she looked irritated.

'I will also not eat if you don't,' saying so, her mother handed over the plate to her.

Swati ate silently.

Swati's cousins came to attend her wedding. They had brought gifts for her – clothes, gold and silver ornaments. Swati's mother got new clothes stitched for all of them.

'We want to meet Swati's husband today,' her sister announced, as her daughter clung to her.

'We would like to go with you,' the children clamoured, curious to see the man Swati would wed.

They went there in the evening. When they pressed the doorbell, an elderly lady, with peppered hair, opened the door.

'Yes?' there was a frown on her face.

'We are Swati's sisters. We want to meet your son.'

'Please come in, ' the frown gave way to a smile as the old lady stepped aside, making way for them.

'Delhi is very cold in December and January,' the old lady observed, wrapping the shawl tightly around herself.

'The sky is overcast. It may rain today.'

'I hope it doesn't rain on the wedding day,' one of the sisters said.

'Where will the wedding take place?'

'In a banquet hall, in Mehrauli.'

The old lady looked relieved.

'My son comes back late at night, around ten to eleven', the old lady continued.

A young maid brought fruit juice for them.

'You know these multinationals; they pay you well, but they make you slog like donkeys.'

'Does your sister know how to cook?'

'She is a great cook. And unlike us, she keeps experimenting.'

'My son is fond of good food,' the old lady informed them. 'With my husband dead, I have showered all my attention on him. He is my only child, and I want him to have a happy marital life.'

The sisters were slightly scared. Swati was hot-tempered, and the lady seemed to be equally so. They fervently hoped the two would live in harmony.

It was a quiet wedding. Fifteen to twenty relatives and friends attended the marriage from the groom's side.

Swati cried, hugging her mother, as she left.

17

Public Shame

Swati's husband was of soft temperament, and treated her well. But she did not get along with his mother. Both were independent-minded women, fiery.

'My son is an alumnus of IIM, Ahmedabad,' the old lady shouted one day, as she folded her son's clothes. While handing them over to the washer man, she muttered, 'He could have married any girl. My son deserved better.'

'I have also done law from Bangalore Law School, the best in the country right now,' Swati retorted. Her mother had warned her; and asked her not to answer back, but she could not help it.

Everyday, when her son came back, the old lady had a long list of complaints. Poor man did not know what to do. He was fond of his mother, and loved his wife. His management skills were quite handy in his office, but not at home.

'What have I become?' his wife would complain. 'I stay at home all day, Ma nagging all the time.'

'Why don't you start going to the court again?' Swati's husband suggested. 'If you are not at home all day, may be you will fight less.'

Swati considered the proposal. She went to her mother in the evening.

'You should be more compromising. One needs to make adjustments in any relationship,' her mother counselled. 'You try to understand that poor woman's predicament. Her husband was dead when she was very young; and all her aspirations have centred around her son.'

'But Ma, I get totally fed up,' Swati continued complaining. 'I have to sit at home all day, listening to the old lady complain about something or the other.'

'I have built my clientele in these few years of practice. I am losing my practice. And I do nothing but listen to my ma-in-law grumble.'

'Why don't you re-join your calling?' Swati's mother suggested. 'Your husband comes home late. Your career will not suffer a setback, and maybe, if you remove yourself from home for a while, you will quarrel less.'

Swati thought of Varun and remained silent.

'Ma, I will think about it.'

Her husband came to their place at ten-thirty at night. He had his dinner with Swati and her mother, as his mother-in-law spoke gently, 'Her clients keep calling up. My daughter had a good practice. She had her own independent briefs, and earned a neat sum every month.'

'She does nothing when at home', Swati's husband responded, 'except for fighting with my mother.' He said this in an undertone.

'I too want her to resume her practice,' he said aloud.

Swati debated whether she should rejoin the profession so early. If she did so, it would mean meeting Varun. And she was in no mood to see him. But she needed to go back to the courts. Getting admission in Bangalore Law School had not been so easy, and she had slogged. She remembered working hard on all her cases. Drafting, filing, arguing, she had done all this. She had acquired some expertise.

But was she ready to face Varun?

At night she went to the nearby Mall with her husband, to watch a movie in the multiplex. They bought the tickets, and waited. The movie was to start after half an hour.

'Shall we buy something I can wear in the courts, now that we have some time?'

Swati's husband agreed to her proposal.

'I want shades in black, white, and grey.' Finally, Swati selected four shades and got them packed. They hurried towards the movie hall. The cast was being shown. The sound was so loud that Swati put her fingers on her ears. By and by, she got accustomed to the high volume. She started enjoying the movie. It was a comedy, with no particular story line. Nevertheless, it was entertaining. Every time something funny was shown, her husband looked at her. Both laughed together.

They bought butter-soaked popcorns, served in large, funnel-shaped paper cones. They munched, watching the movie with interest.

It was around midnight when they were at the parking lot. Swati hummed a song. She was in good mood. Her husband unrolled the mirror, paid the man at the parking. Then drove off.

Delhi looked dark, and beautiful. The roads were long and straight, with streetlights. Swati was lost in her own thoughts. She was thinking of her future, and was apprehensive.

Swati started going to the court again. She felt better. Her husband dropped her, on way to his office. Now her mother-in-law had less complaints against her, and she also had less time to fight. The two women had their tea together in the evening, in their garden. When Swati reached her house, she would see her mother-in-law watering the grass, and the flowers. She would ask the small girl, their domestic help, to bring chairs for them in the lawn. They would sit there, sip their tea, and talk. At times her mother-in-law would complain about their neighbour. Swati gave her a patient hearing. She was more tolerant now that she was out of the house the entire day. She spent less time at home. The old lady was also more understanding now. Sometimes the old lady observed that Swati had a mixed expression on her face when she talked. She had a vague feeling something was worrying her daughter-in-law.

One day the old lady talked to her son.

'I have seen the world,' she observed, 'something is killing your wife. Talk to your wife about it.'

Swati's husband knew his wife struggled with something, but he could not exactly pinpoint. When he saw her sit up all night, with a book in hand, its pages unturned, he knew something was amiss. He was waiting for her to tell him; but apparently, she did not want to.

Once as Swati sat, the *Supreme Court Reporter* on her lap, her head propped against the chair, her husband sat close to her. He shut her book.

Swati looked up.

'Why do you pretend you are reading when your thoughts are elsewhere?'

She was startled.

'Tomorrow I have to argue a matter. I am doing research.'

'Relax. Don't overstrain yourself.'

Swati noted down the citations. Her husband could see she had copied everything wrong. He moved away, not wanting to embarrass his wife.

Swati met Varun in the corridor the next day. She looked away. He came closer to her.

'I want to talk to you.'

She looked at him questioningly.

She met Varun at the parking lot. She sat beside him, silently. Varun drove off. They reached a secluded place. He parked his car under a tree, in the shade. Small, half-naked children ran around nearby. Varun stretched himself on his seat, and looked at Swati. He smiled. Swati gave him a faint smile. Emboldened, he stooped. He started kissing her passionately on her breasts. Swati responded. Her hair was dishevelled.

Suddenly they saw a man advance towards them. He banged at their car.

'Open the door,' he shouted.

More men started converging. Swati and Varun were surrounded by ten to twelve men, all able bodied. They threw angry looks at them.

'Lock him inside,' one of them shouted, 'and call the police.'

'I am coming out,' Varun said, pleading with them.

'Could you not find any other place for doing all this?'

'I am sorry,' he pleaded again, 'let us go.'

Swati was sitting quietly. Her heart beat fast, and she sweated. Surprisingly, public wrath was directed at Varun. They said nothing to her.

'Call the police,' one of them shouted.

The police van came in five minutes.

'You are a lawyer. You should know doing these things in public is an offence.'

'I am sorry. Please pardon me.'

Swati's husband was called.

'So you are her husband,' the policeman looked at him mockingly. 'Your wife was caught with this man, doing things on road you would disapprove of.'

Varun looked at Swati's husband nervously.

'Let my wife go,' her husband spoke coolly.

The policeman took Varun inside. Swati could see Varun hand over a wad of currency notes, which the policeman pocketed. There was a look of satisfaction on his face.

The policeman leered at Swati as she left.

Swati went with her husband, a look of shame on her face. What had she done? She wanted to forget the past, but it clung to her. She never intended to be intimate with Varun again. She did not have the courage to look at her husband. What will he think? What kind of woman had he married? She wanted to hide her face.

As her husband parked his car in the garage, her mother-in-law appeared. Her hair was wet.

'You are back so early! And you two have come together!'

'Ma, we want to see a movie, and then would go for dinner. We decided to take a break.'

His mother nodded.

Both left the house after an hour. Swati did not speak. They went to a restaurant, and ordered cold coffee. As she sipped her coffee, she felt her husband looked at her intently.

'Tell me everything, right from the beginning,' he spoke, holding her hand.

Swati shivered. She spoke rapidly, as words tumbled out. She laid bare her relationship with her senior.

'At times you wanted to know what bothered me. This is what had been bothering me. My past. I was frightened you would know of it, and leave me. And now you know everything.'

There was a look of exasperation on Swati's face. Her eyes bore the expression of a fear that ate her.

Her husband smiled.

'I am not going to let go of such a wife so easily.'

She could not believe her ears. She had not anticipated this response.

She felt hungry.

'I have ordered chicken biryani,' her husband said, looking at her kindly. She bit into the leg of the chicken, as the flesh stuck to her teeth. She had felt so hungry after months. It seemed she was free of shackles, nothing bothered her now.

Swati stood up, and hugged her husband. Others looked on.

She was not bothered.

During weekend, Swati's husband dropped her at her parents. Her father was worried.

'Are things between you and your mother-in-law alright?'

Swati smiled.

'Why do you worry? We get along quite well.'

'And how are things on professional front?'

'I work hard on all my briefs. The clients' interest is uppermost in my mind.'

'There is no short cut to success. Hard work pays.'

Swati nodded.

'And listen, my child,' her father continued, with a slight smile, 'you have been our favourite daughter, brilliant and hard working.'

Swati wondered how her father would react if he came to know of her past, especially about the recent incident involving Varun and herself.

Swati looked away.

Her mother had not changed the décor of her room, nor had she touched her things. The clothes she had left behind were still in cupboard, all her jeans and T-shirts hanging in a row. Her novels were on shelves, and her mother took care to dust them everyday.

One day Swati sprang when she picked up one of her novels. She had inserted a picture of Varun and herself amongst its pages. She had hidden it, putting it behind the row of clothes. At night when every one was asleep, she pulled out the photograph. They had requested one of the passersby to click them when they had gone to India Gate, one evening. Varun looked at her fondly, as she stood there. Her face was pressed against his.

After dinner Swati latched her bedroom from inside, and pulled out the photograph. She looked at it for some time. Then she tore it, and threw the shreds in the dustbin.

Varun had gifted an expensive bottle of perfume to her. She went to the washbasin, and emptied its contents. She threw the empty bottle, sat down, and started crying soundlessly.

She switched on her PC. It was full of e-mails she had received from Varun, expressing his yearning for her.

Normally Varun sat on his PC much after midnight, after he had finished with his professional work. He sent Swati e-mails. She deleted each one of them. She wanted Varun out of her system.

She had gone on tours with Varun. They had stayed together in a single room. Unknown faces had seen them together.

She tried recollecting the faces of innumerable airhostesses, the waiters, the ushers and hundred of others who had seen them together. Her husband was quick to ignore her past, but that did not necessarily mean she was rid of it.

She had seen her mother look at her strangely once when she had come back after spending a night with Varun. She could see her mother sniffing. Swati had gone to her room and removed her dress. It had smelled of after shave.

E-mails could be deleted, but memories did not fade easily.

Her mother came to her, with an affectionate look on her face. 'Your sisters keep asking about you.' She spread out a bunch of clothes that had come by parcel.

Swati looked at the bundle. There were beautiful *sarees*, bed sheets and bedcovers, all embroidered. Swati was touched.

'Come down,' her mother said gently, 'your father has brought *gulab jamuns* for you.'

Swati came down. Her father was heating the *gulab jamuns* for her.

'Leave it, papa, I will do it,' she had said, moving close to her father.

'We feel very lonely. Why don't you come and see us more often?'

'I come here every weekend,' Swati looked at her father reproachfully.

Her husband came in the evening. After dinner, when they were about to go, Swati's mother handed over a tiffin to her.

'This is for your mother-in-law,' she said. 'She need not cook for herself.'

Swati knew she had to get up early the next day. She wanted to go home and sleep early.

Her mother-in-law liked the gesture. She immediately rang up and thanked Swati's mother.

'You cook so well. Your daughter has learnt her culinary skills from you.' Swati's mother went to sleep with a satisfied look on her face. 'Thank God, the two get along well now,' she sighed.

As Swati was changing, her husband stared at her. He came to her. He did not utter a word, as he disrobed his wife.

'I can see why your boss was mad about you, dear,' he whispered into her ears, stroking her thighs. His eyes were hot with passion. He was behaving with ferocity. He was biting her all over, as if he wanted to tear the flesh off her body.

Swati tried to push him away, looking at him fearfully.

'No, let me have what is rightfully mine,' he pounced on Swati, crushing her in his arms.

Swati shrieked.

Swati suffocated under his weight. He was brutal. He was in no mood to show mercy. Anger possessed him.

They hardly spoke to each other for the next two days. Swati went to the court and attended to her matters listlessly. She met Mr. Kaul, a colleague, in the Main Library one day as she was stooping over the book, *Law of Crimes*.

'Doing research?' Mr. Kaul pulled a chair, sitting beside her.

Swati nodded. She was in no mood to talk to anyone.

'I met Varun's wife in the Andamans. She had come on vacation with a young lady.'

Why is he telling me?

Swati got up, and left.

She was relieved her mother-in-law was not at home. She had a splitting headache. The whole world seemed to know of her relationship with Varun.

A soft breeze blew, she felt a cooling sensation. She asked the maid to prepare a strong cup of ginger flavoured tea. After finishing tea she got up, and started removing weeds from around the rose bushes. The tender branches trembled as a strong gust of wind blew. She bent and smelled one of the roses. Tiny pots, hanging from trees, looked pretty. Towards the corner, she had upturned three four pots, put a marble slab on them, and placed some potted plants there. They looked pretty, bringing freshness to her garden. Swati yearned to be left alone amongst those flowers and plants. She fervently wished her mother-in-law came back late. She wanted her husband to be detained in his office.

Swati wished the clock turned a few years ahead of time. She wanted to forget this phase of her life.

The maid walked up to her.

'It is quite dark, memsahib. Why don't you come in and watch television? Ammaji will come back late.'

'I am perfectly alright here,' she replied.

Swati started walking along the hedges, feeling cold wind on her face. She felt she needed to mow the lawn.

At around nine, her mother-in-law came back. She looked tired, and fell on the chair.

Swati brought a chilled glass of water.

'Ms. Bagga's daughter is to be engaged tomorrow,' she said. 'I was with her to help her in the preparations.'

She listened to her mother-in-law silently.

'I will have to go back,' the old lady said. 'Poor Ms. Bagga is not able to handle it alone. I will stay with her the whole night and help her out.'

The old woman had her dinner in a hurry, and left. Swati shut the door, relieved that she was alone once again. She came back to the comforts of her garden.

Swati felt at peace with the world as she remembered the might of God.

Her husband came back at one in the morning. He had his dinner in the office. He took out his clothes, wrapped a towel, and went to the bathroom. After a quick shower, he came back, droplets of water clinging to his body. He changed into a fresh night suit and came to Swati. She pretended she was sleeping, as her husband cradled her in his arms, and kissed her gently.

Swati did not open her eyes. She apprehended that her husband would behave with her savagely.

He was gentle with her, holding her with the same tenderness one holds a baby.

He went off to sleep, his wife in his arms.

Things were getting normal.

Varun met Swati again, in the courtroom. Swati tried to ignore him, moving past him, showing no signs of recognition. He came closer to her, and whispered,

'I need to talk to you.'

Swati glared at him.

'I thought everything was over.'

Varun grinned sheepishly, 'That day it was very embarrassing. That bastard took a fat sum from me.'

'Anyway, Simran is not coming back. And I feel quite lonely. I miss you.'

The man was incorrigible. Just because his wife refused to join him, he was interested in her.

'So your wife was in Andamans.'

'Who told you?' There was a look of disbelief in Varun's eyes.

'The world is small.'

'I want to have lunch with you.'

'I am carrying my lunch.'

'You know everything is over,' this time she was firm. 'Why do you keep bothering me?'

'Who says everything is over? At least not from my side.'

'How can you be so shameless?' saying so Swati left.

She proceeded towards the canteen and ordered a Sprite. She sat there, a solitary figure, looking at nothing in particular.

'Ma'am, anything else?' the waiter stood before her.

'Get me a plate of samosas,' she said in an indifferent tone. Swati ordered another plate, and ate hungrily. One of her colleagues smiled at her. They had worked under the same senior for two years, before Swati joined Varun. She was still working under the same senior, while Swati was independent.

Was this independence worth it? Did it not come with a cost?

Her colleague joined her. 'My matters are over,' she said, 'and I do not intend to go to the office before six.'

'I had only one case. It has been adjourned,' Swati said.

'Let us go to the Trade Fair. We can buy some junk jewellery.'

Swati agreed. Both the women entered the Gujarati and Rajasthani pavilions, and bought some colourful bracelets and pendants.

Swati bought a shawl for her mother-in-law, embroidered in pink and white. They went to Good Living, jostled past the crowd, and reached enclosures selling electronic goods. She took the card of a salesman, who demonstrated microwave ovens. She would talk to her husband when he came back. They needed a microwave.

'Does your husband know about Varun?' Swati was shocked, when her colleague asked her. She had been discreet about her relationship with Varun, but it seemed everyone was aware of it.

'Yes,' she said curtly.

'How did he react to it?'

That was the problem with women. They were more interested in what the other woman did.

'Are you married?' Swati asked.

'Yes,' her colleague looked surprised.

'Did I ask you what your husband had for lunch today?'

Her colleague was taken aback. She was not prepared for this.

She came back, sulking. Flinging her purse on a side table, she sprawled on the bed. Her past was like a shadow that never left her. She desperately wished she became a fresh graduate, just out of the Law School. She could have started life afresh, on a clean slate.

18

Anguish

It had not been so easy for Swati's husband. He had acted with composure before his wife. But his mind was in great tumult.

He walked on the roads of Delhi, aimlessly. He touched his engagement ring, again and again. He felt he was touching Swati. He shuddered. His wife had a past. He knew. Why was it so painful? Why could he not just forget it?

A naked child ran on the road as a speeding car screeched to a halt.

Why are relationships full of complexities? Why cannot things be simpler? He adored her, loved the way she smiled, laughed, frowned. Suddenly he had an urge to strangle her; to get on top of her, and asphyxiate her. He had trusted her, she had breached his faith.

Swati and he hardly quarrelled. Swati had remained aloof most of the time, lost in her own thoughts. He envied those who had fights.

Swati was not quite fond of socializing, and she spoke little. Most of the time she replied in monosyllables. She often gave him a slight smile.

What had she seen in her senior? He was a middle aged man with a grown up son.

He felt he had much more to offer.

Women were treacherous creatures. He did not understand them. He had seen Swati kiss the sheet on which he had written. She had said she loved touching the paper on which he wrote.

And she went out with Varun.

He hated it when he remembered what the policeman had said. He had stood by his wife in public. He did not intend to belittle her. And he hated himself for doing so. What exactly did she want? She had celebrated his birthday a few days ago. She had presented a watch to him. She ensured that the day was special. He was overwhelmed. No one had made this day so special for him. And she looked dazzling in white tussar silk. She wore the ornaments tastefully, looking strikingly beautiful.

It was getting slightly chilly. He put both his hands in his pockets. He had buttoned his shirt, right up to his throat. He tossed his hair and took quick steps. He did not want to go home. The walls looked at him with mocking eyes.

He could not bear the humiliation.

He wanted to die.

He got a call from Swati. She sounded depressed. Maybe she had cried. He knew Varun's shadow lurked somewhere. His wife could not forget him so easily. She cried for someone else. He was jealous. He was her man. She had no business to feel for someone else. If she felt for him so much, why did she not go to him? Varun had refused to commit, he knew. He wondered why his wife was involved with someone so heartless. Had he been in her place, he would have kicked Varun on his shins.

A man walked ahead of him. He had quickened his pace, seemed to be in a hurry to reach home.

Swati's husband was in no such hurry.

He worked hard, saved. He wanted to build a beautiful house for his wife. It all seemed so worthless now.

Men are simple. They are easy to understand. It is different with women. When Swati went into a shell, he tried to cheer her up. He sang, joked. He spared no effort to make her feel special.

At times he was exasperated. What is the problem with these women? You do things for them, and they behave as if they are God's gift to men. When he tried cheering her up, she got up and walked up to the verandah. She looked at the sky listlessly.

Most of the time he ignored her mood swings. He could see she behaved more weirdly ever since she had started going to the courts again. Anyway, the fights with his mother had become less frequent.

He was a busy man in the office. He had to give presentations, meet deadlines. He chatted with his colleagues during coffee breaks. After a hard day's work, he looked forward to meeting his wife and his mother. Nothing cheered him more than a cup of tea which he had with his family when he was back from work. He had a tough boss, who gave him impossible deadlines. He hated it when his boss found fault with his work. He would be bombarded with e-mails after every five minutes. He felt he needed to switch over to some other company.

He was frustrated in his office, he was frustrated at home.

He touched his engagement ring again and again. When he had worn it for the first time, he felt a part of him was linked to Swati forever.

He looked at the ring disdainfully. It was like a serpent on his finger. He took out the ring and put it in his pocket.

He had a wife he could depend on. He knew if he were in trouble she would stand by him. She was one of those who gave strength during adversity. She would not panic, would not buckle under pressure. He had been impressed by her intellect.

Swati had a past! He felt like throttling her.

He kicked a pebble; watching intently as the pebble hit the ground. He kicked it, again and again, remembering Swati.

He reached home. Swati looked at him silently as he took out his shoes and socks and went off to sleep.

19

Varun Calls Up

Simran was in Chennai. She was restless. Memories which she was keen to forget, flooded back to her. She took her classes absentmindedly. Mary rang her up once or twice a week. She was in the advanced stage of pregnancy, and looked completely round. Once when she had come to spend a day with Simran, Praseetha Amma advised her, 'You should take more fruits and green, leafy vegetables. Pregnancy is like penance, you need to take care of yourself and the baby.'

Mary listened to Praseetha Amma intently.

'Do take sprouts regularly, rich in folic acid,' Simran also butted in. 'It is good for the child's brain.'

Mary nodded.

Simran was marking the answer sheets. Final examinations had taken place and piles of answer sheets lay on her table. She wanted to drown herself in work.

At times she could be seen, at two in the morning, busy in her work.

She had also started going to other colleges, as a guest speaker, to deliver lectures on select topics. Students listened to her when she spoke. She had taken up the task of editing books on her subject. By now she had become a known figure in the academic circle in Chennai. She had also started writing commentaries in newspapers on select issues, which were appreciated.

Varun came to Chennai one day, by the evening flight. Sunita opened the door, her hands covered with flour. When she saw Varun, she ran inside, shouting,

'Sahib has come.'

Simran was sitting in her study, making notes. Sunita ran to her.

'Sahab has come,' she came, panting.

Varun was sitting in the living room, a magazine in his hands. He looked at Simran when she entered the room. She was in pyjamas, with boxes in purple and white. She had cut her hair short, and looked younger.

Varun looked fatigued.

'I had a hectic day,' he said, smiling at his wife, 'I had to run to catch the flight.'

Sunita brought a chilled glass of Pepsi. Setting it on the side table, she ran back to the kitchen. She knew Varun loved pizzas, and wanted to check whether the ingredients were at home.

'I am going to the market,' saying so she went out. She ran back. Placing her buy on the kitchen slab, she chopped capsicum, carrot, and onion.

'Isn't the tandoor working?' Simran asked, as she saw Sunita work hard in the kitchen.

'Yes memsahib, I had called the electrician yesterday. It is now in order.'

Varun followed Simran to the kitchen, his hands in his pockets.

'Give that to me,' he said, 'I will grate cheese.'

In ten minutes, they prepared the dinner.

Sunita looked happy. 'Had Bunny baba been here, we would have had more fun.'

'We will talk to Bunny,' Simran said softly, dialling her son's number.

No one took the call. Bunny was asleep.

Varun and Simran went for a walk after dinner. Varun spoke a lot, and Simran listened. She hardly spoke. Looking at the road ahead, he said, 'I am lonely without you.'

Simran remained silent. She remembered William, and wondered if he ever felt lonely without her. Did the man she had loved so passionately ever remember her? Sunita had told her, when enquired, that the man who came to the lady's house was none other than Mary's brother. During evenings he told his sister that he went to a friend's for night stay. Though their mother disapproved, William did not bother. He made regular trips to Chennai.

Simran had listened with her head bowed. She never had the courage to speak to Mary directly, about her brother.

She had no inclination to go with Varun.

'Your friends miss you, they keep asking about you.'

Simran thought vaguely of Ms. Mishra.

'Brigadier Singh's wife always cooks and sends over something for me. She always asks me to get you back.'

'How is her granddaughter?'

'Ms. Singh has brought her back to Delhi. She could not live without Cookie, neither could the child.'

They continued walking, as wind blew.

'Do you really need me?'

There was a pause.

'Has Swati left you?'

Varun looked at his wife. How much did she know?

'Actually, Swati does not need to work under me any longer. She has her independent briefs and has started practicing on her own.'

Simran looked at the road ahead, wondering if Varun and Swati had split. They took a turn. When they were a young couple they had walked for hours after dinner, but invariably they had come back fighting. Simran was then young and rash. She fought tooth and nail, opposing Varun on almost every issue. But now she was tired. She had neither the energy nor the will to fight. She had given up.

Once Simran had gone to Varun's office. Swati was working, her head bowed. In her presence Varun called Swati and showed her the mistakes she had committed. He had shouted at her, pointing towards each mistake, admonishing her. Simran could see Swati cringe as she stood there. She was asked to go after a few minutes. When Simran left the office, she could see a tiny tear drop cling to Swati's cheek.

Simran laughed inwardly. Why did her husband have to put up this pretence every time she saw him with Swati? What was he trying to prove? Was he trying to please one at the expense of the other? Men can be so disgusting at times.

Simran went away, a look of disgust on her face.

Varun said presently, 'You seem to be quite busy nowadays, editing books, writing in the periodicals.'

'I think it is time to go back.'

They turned back towards their house.

Suddenly Simran's heart skipped a beat. She saw William, a few steps ahead of her. Intuitively, William turned around, and he was shocked when he saw Simran. The two looked at each other, speechless.

Varun had quickened his pace. He needed to go to the washroom, and hurried back. Simran trailed behind him.

She thought she would collapse. William was walking very close to her. She could almost touch him.

Had he nothing to say? Did she not deserve a few words of explanation from him?

'I did not know you were in Chennai,' William spoke finally, his hands in his pockets. He pulled out a handkerchief and wiped his face.

Simran staggered. William caught her, and pulled her to a bench, under the tree. Simran saw Varun press the doorbell, and rush inside their house. She was perspiring profusely, her hands were clammy. William held her, supporting her in the crook of his arm. She swooned.

When she regained her senses, she found herself in her bedroom. Varun sat beside her, reading a newspaper.

'No, don't get up,' he instructed, 'you had fainted.'

Varun continued, 'A passerby saw you and carried you home.'

Simran felt her head was throbbing. A passerby! So that is how William had introduced himself.

'I may have to go back by the evening flight tomorrow,' her husband spoke as he folded the newspaper carefully. There were lines on his face.

Varun stood before the mirror, to shave. There was stubble on his face. He had not shaved for the past two days. When Swati was with him, she shaved him. She said it was a great turn on for her. Varun remembered her as he turned on the tap, the razor in his hand. He felt a sudden urge to be with her, feel her soft hands on his cheeks. He felt a certain tenderness towards his ex-junior. She had loved him, she was ready to face the world for him. But he had buckled. Suddenly he had remembered his wife, and felt he had his duty towards her. Had he been supportive and willing, he was sure, Swati would have run away with him. He had not stood by her. He had spoken to her harshly. He had a feeling Swati felt she had been used.

But had she not used him? She got her briefs at such a young age because of him. Lawyers of her standing still struggled in the profession, but she had done well.

And, Varun felt, Swati was better off without him. There was an age gap of almost twenty years between them. It was alright till she was in love with him, but once that was over, she would have certainly repented her decision. Bunny had become an adult, he was not a problem. But somehow, however much he told Swati that life had become beautiful after she had entered his life, Varun knew he was not the man for her.

One can have sex with any woman, but for an enduring relationship, other things do matter.

Swati was not homely. She had a mind of her own. She was ambitious, she could do anything to achieve her goal. Simran may not have given him much sexual satisfaction, but she was his kind. They had the same kind of background. And at this age, Varun was in no mood to experiment. He liked experimenting only in his sexual life.

Simran had gone to the bathroom. Varun sat on the bed, waiting for her. He had decided, no one could take his wife's place. She had loved him, and stood by him for almost two decades, and at this age he could not think of leaving her. She had been his support.

Varun took the evening flight and reached Delhi, late at night. His driver was at the airport, to receive him. He reached home, and switched on the television. He was about to change the channel. He stopped. Swati was on television, being interviewed. She had fought a case for the custody of a child successfully, and was telling the reporter what the court had ordered. Her client stood near her, happy that the child would finally be hers. Hmmmm, she looks smart, he thought, as he saw Swati give the interview confidently. He wanted her in his arms.

'Well done,' he congratulated Swati the next day when he met her in the courtroom. 'You got your client a good order.'

Swati said thanks and walked away. She laughed softly. She could not protect her own turf, and there she was, being congratulated as the champion of some one else's right.

Life has its mysteries. When she saw the judges in the courtroom one day, dispensing justice, she had a vague feeling they had all been cheated at some point of time. But there they were, sitting and deciding cases for someone's rights.

Swati was determined. She would work hard and succeed. Then she would look disdainfully at the one who had cheated her, and make him cringe. She did not want to wallow in self pity.

The client had come to her office in the evening with a box of sweets. 'It was all your effort,' she wiped her tears, as she spoke. The child had been her lifeline. She would have died had she not got the custody of the child. Swati had not known motherhood, but she could feel the anguish of a mother when separated from her child.

When she returned home, her mother-in-law smiled, and welcomed her.

'We saw you on television,' she was beaming.

Swati felt exhausted. She turned on the tap and washed her feet with cold water. She wanted her mind to be blank. She wanted to think of nothing. But memories flooded her mind. Varun rejecting her as she sat, almost pleading with him, the look of harshness on his face. Her husband humiliating her, treating her body with harshness. She cringed. And she was called a champion of women's rights by the reporter, as he introduced her to the viewers. She laughed aloud.

Her mother-in-law knocked.

Varun came to Swati's chamber next morning. His eyes were bloodshot.

'You are drinking hard,' she said, marking out the relevant lines with a marker. Varun leaned over the table, and whispered, 'When our women leave us, this is how we try to cope.'

'I have a case in court no. three,' she said after a while, 'I should prepare.'

Varun rose and left.

He went to the Bar Room and tried to read a newspaper. Soon he gave up. He had tried to please the two women in his life. Both had turned him down. He had almost pleaded with Simran to come back, but to no avail. She had lost interest in him, it was evident.

He had loved Swati. But he had jilted her as he was reminded of his duty towards his wife.

Both the women nursed a grievance against him. He wanted to please both. He had been able to please neither. The success that Swati had was due to him. He had trained her, taught her law. He had given her exposure, got her cases. The confidence with which she handled her own cases was due to him.

Simran wanted to go to Chennai. She was bored of him. He had not objected to it. He had made arrangements for her well being. He had been a dutiful father, sending over money to his son regularly. Bunny had never complained to his mother about anything. Yet, Varun felt alone, isolated, rejected.

Bunny had come over for the weekend. They went to the club, swam, and played tennis. Bunny was building his career, and talked of nothing else. Somewhere, deep within, Varun thought his son had also felt that he had cheated his mother.

Varun put the newspaper on the table. He went to the canteen and ordered a hot cup of ginger tea. Swati had no qualms about taking obligations from him, but now she behaved as if she was the wronged one.

Varun had his tea, and made the payment. He walked up to the parking lot. Putting his coat in the hanger, he rolled his gown and placed it at the back seat. He drove off.

It was cloudy, the wind howled. The doors banged and the windows rattled. He shut all the windows of his house. Had Simran or Swati been there, they would have managed everything. He sat on the terrace.

It rained. The park was filled with water. Varun saw a spark of lightning, followed by thunder. He envied Swati's husband. As it rained hard, his desire to be with her grew. She had given him the pleasures he had not known for years. He had felt guilty when he thought of his wife, but wasn't it human? After all, he had worked hard to provide for his family for years. Was he being too selfish if he snatched a few moments for himself?

Varun was irritated. Women were strange creatures. They only knew how to throw tantrums and poor men had to bear them. Modern day women wanted all the freedoms of life.

Simran earned enough, and so did Swati. Both did what they pleased. Simran left him to go to Chennai, and Swati came to him of her own free will. He remembered the first time when he had touched Swati. He had been slightly scared. He felt very thirsty when Swati stood very close to him. He had dared and pressed her hand slightly. Swati could have objected. She did not. He sat down, and talked of his sexual life with his wife. Swati showed interest. If she wanted, she could have put a stop to everything. When he had asked those in the office to leave so that he could be alone with Swati, she had not objected. He felt her all over. She had responded, clinging to him, placing her head on his shoulders. Not once did she object when he took her on trips to various cities, in India and abroad. They had stayed in the same rooms, drinking, making love. Swati got as much pleasure as he did. She had moaned, she had shrieked with sheer pleasure when he had her. It was a two–way street.

Why are women such emotional fools? Why do they cry at the slightest pretext? Why don't they understand that life was for pleasure, not for shedding tears? One would have expected such modern women as Simran and Swati to be more level-headed. Both went all the way, and then started behaving as if they were the ones who were wronged.

Swati always felt Varun humiliated her in front of his wife. His motive was to ensure that Simran did not get suspicious of their relationship. She deeply resented it and did not talk to him for several days. Varun had to really make an effort to please her.

Varun made a drink for himself. He poured whisky in a wide mouthed glass. He asked the maid to prepare some kebabs for him.

The maid peeped inside. Varun asked her to get some more kebabs. The maid wrinkled her nose as she came close to Varun. He smelled of alcohol.

Varun was a successful man. Success had not come to him within a day. He had worked hard for it. He had spent nights preparing for his matters, and had slogged in the offices of his seniors till late hours. He was not a pretty face for whom success came easily. And at this age, he wanted to relax, and enjoy life. He had given the golden period of his life struggling, did he not deserve some pleasure?

Varun was on his couch, staring at his empty bedroom. He wanted Swati in his arms. He took a pillow and clutched it tightly. That woman had started giving him sleepless nights. Every time he imagined her with her husband, he was terribly jealous. Varun remembered Swati, shedding all her clothes within five minutes of her coming to his house. She had fun along with him. The problem arose when she started getting sentimental.

It was 2 a.m. in the morning. Varun picked up his mobile and searched for Swati's number. No one received the call. Varun rang up again. Swati saw his number. She got up stealthily, and leaving the bedroom, she talked in a hushed tone.

'What is the matter?'

'I want you,' his voice slurred, as he spoke unsteadily.

'At 2 a.m.? Have you gone mad?'

'Yes, I have gone mad. I want you with me right now.'

'Shut up!' saying so, she hung up.

She felt very irritated. When she was ready to leave everything and go to him, he had failed her. Now when she was trying to build her own life, he was trying to get entry into her life. Why couldn't he decide what he wanted? And did he think he could leave and get her whenever he wanted?

Swati could not sleep. She had spent nights with the man, giving him pleasure. And what had she wanted in return? A permanent relationship, nothing less. She remembered Varun telling her that Simran had left him as she was bored, and wanted a change in life. 'She has left me of her own free will,' he often said. 'I don't think she is interested in me any longer.' Swati had wanted to fill that void. She was interested in him. Despite the wide age gap, she was happy to be with him. And what had he said! 'You should have thought before thinking of a relationship with a married man.'

She opened the refrigerator and pulled out a bottle of water. She drank water in gulps. She did not return to her bedroom. She went to her study and hid herself behind a thick book. Swati was smart and intelligent. She could have married any man of her choice, but she had chosen Varun. But the man had rejected her. When she remembered the incident when they had to go to the police station, her humiliation was complete. Swati, a highly educated woman, had to suffer humiliation at the hands of a bunch of semi-educated men. When she remembered the policemen leering at her, she went red. Swati cursed herself. And look at the man! He had the guts to ring her up at this time and talk to her so! Why did he not leave her alone and run to his wife? The man was obnoxious.

Suddenly Swati found her husband lean over her.

'You are holding the book upside down,' he observed, lighting a cigarette.

'Had Varun called up?' he was asking, the smell of tobacco filling the room.

Swati nodded.

'Do you want to drink tea?' she asked her husband.

'Yes.'

Both went to the kitchen and prepared tea together.

They did not sleep that night.

20

The Old Woman

William visited Mary on a windy day. The sky was overcast, clouds were like smudges on a child's canvas. Mary had a tiny garden which she tended to with care. Despite her bulging belly, she sat on a low stool, and pulled out the weeds. William had brought some fresh saplings for her. While William sat on his haunches, handing over each sapling to his sister, the latter sat on her stool, planting them on the edges of her lawn. Each sapling bore a single flower, at the centre. It looked pretty. All the saplings stood in a row, the flowers adding colour to the garden.

Mary continued sitting on her stool, as William pulled a chair and sat beside her.

'William,' his sister spoke, her hands still occupied, 'did you love Simran?'

William looked at his sister intently; he did not speak for a while.

'I had a feeling she loved you, and was going through emotional trauma. Often, in our conversation, I sensed she looked at me not as her friend, but as your sister.'

As William thought of Simran, her stately figure, and the sharp, aquiline nose flashed across his mind. William had been fascinated by her; a fair skinned, North Indian woman, exuding confidence, and walking with poise.

He had dreamt of her, imagining her soft body in his arms. He had confided in a friend from Sothavilai, 'She is so beautiful,' he had told him, 'she has the kind of classic features one finds rarely.'

His friend had laughed.

'Do you realize she is older than you? She is your guest, treat her as one. Do not think of anything beyond that.'

It was the memory of Simran that made him sad. Simran had clung to him, trusted him. Simran, whom he stroked, petted, and loved, as the waves crashed against the tree to which they clung.

How could he forget her, someone who had entered his system?

He saw Mary look at him impatiently.

'Why don't you speak?'

William remembered the day he had seen Simran walking with a man, presumably her husband. They had cut a striking figure as they walked ahead of him. He felt a rush of blood on his face when he saw the woman walk ahead of him. He had a sudden urge to stop her. They took a turn. William had quickened his pace. He wanted to see Simran. He saw her walk alone as her husband took quick strides, and disappeared in darkness.

He moved closer. Simran turned; her face turned white when she saw William, who stood before her, his eyes searching hers. He had tried to talk to her; she was in shock. When he smiled, and extended his hands, she collapsed.

William was in a fix. He held her in his arms and carried her to a wooden bench. He moved her face side wards. He kissed her slightly parted lips. There was no response. She had fainted.

William was frightened. What if anything happened to her? How would he explain to her husband? He did not have time to lose. He carried her on his shoulders and rang her doorbell.

A young woman opened the door. She rushed inside when she saw Simran come back with a stranger. Soon she came back with the man who had walked ahead of him, sometime back.

She had collapsed on the pavement, William was telling him, as her husband helped him put her on her bed.

'Have a drink,' her husband offered when he was leaving.

William refused, and left.

Simran's husband's voice was audible as he rang up a doctor, requesting him to come over to their house urgently.

He remembered walking up to Marilyn's house in a daze. Her daughter opened the door. She brought him a glass of water. Marilyn walked in, carrying a tray, with freshly cut fruits and a glass of orange juice.

William looked at Marilyn. She had enormous eyes. Marilyn looked like an experienced woman. But she looked faded.

William had loved Marilyn. He had loved her desperately. When Marilyn was packing her suitcase, as she had decided to settle in the US, his heart ached. He could not go with her, he had his mother and three younger sisters. Now it was different.

Marilyn wanted William. She was disillusioned with her two failed marriages, and she felt William was her man. She wanted him to come to her.

William had not agreed to her suggestion. He could not stay with her. But he would visit her occasionally. Marilyn rang up whenever William took a long time to come to Chennai.

Mary gave a hard look to her brother. Twice she had asked her brother, twice he had refused to answer her.

She went inside. Her feet were swollen. She wanted to take rest. William followed her to her bedroom.

'Mary,' he said, 'can you ask Simran to come to your house tomorrow, in the evening. I want to meet her.'

'Alright,' she answered, placing her legs on pillows.

'Tomorrow, at what time?' she asked, searching for the remote control, to switch on the television.

'Maybe at six.' Simran is back by two in the afternoon. Six should suit her.

William had decided to stay with his sister for the next few days. In Sothavilai, Matilda was with their mother. Matilda was recovering, William was relieved to see her smile. His mother had distributed the dresses and toys of Agnes to poor children. When she saw the children play with her daughter's toys, she remembered Agnes.

The fishermen went back to the sea. With the help of the government and some N.G.O.s, they were attempting to stand on their feet. William helped them in buying new boats and nets, procure loans from banks on easy terms.

At nights, when retiring, William thought of Simran. He woke up at two in the morning, at three in the morning, thinking of her. Simran looking away as his smouldering eyes fell on her, Simran shrieking as he held her tightly.

She gave him pleasure, and pain.

Simran was in her study when Mary rang the doorbell. Simran had a half-filled mug in her hands; she was sipping tea.

She liked Mary, she was welcome in her home; though she was a bit surprised to see the young woman come at such an early hour.

Sunita brought tea with biscuits.

'The baby is struggling to come out,' Simran smiled, pointing towards her round belly.

'Could you find out whether it is a girl or a boy?'

'Legally, I am not supposed to know the sex of the child, but I have an intuition it will be a baby girl.'

'Shall I name her Simran?'

'But you are a Christian.'

'Her father is a Hindu.'

Sunita came to the room, and switched off the fan. She started cleaning and mopping the floor.

'When Bunny baba was born, I had taken care of him,' she sat on her haunches, holding the mop. 'You call me when your child is born. I will take care of him.'

Mary smiled.

She sat closer to Simran.

'I have come on purpose,' she said softly, looking at Simran.

'William wants to meet you,' she continued.

Simran remained quiet. She did not know how to respond.

'At six in the evening, you come to my place. My brother will be there.'

A few months ago, Simran had painted an earthen pot. She had painted small flowers in red and blue, with its outline in white. At the base, she had painted small figures. The pot looked beautiful, and she had placed it on the refrigerator.

She decided to paint another such pot and give it to William.

Sunita came with a glass of milk, and placed it beside Mary.

Mary smiled, and started taking small sips.

'So, is your husband excited about the baby?'

Simran looked cheerful. She was on the bed, and placing a pillow on her lap, she was talking to Mary animatedly.

'He is more excited than I am. He cannot wait any longer.'

'I hope it is a normal delivery. Caesarean has its own complications.'

'I had caesarean when Bunny was born,' Simran reminisced, 'and I remained clutching at my stomach for one full week, when I had to move.'

As Mary bit into an apple, she questioned, 'Did you gain weight after your son was born?'

'Almost ten kilos. But eventually I shed the extra flab. Child rearing is strenuous and when your energies are directed towards bringing up the child, it can be very tiring.'

When Mary left, it was late in the morning. Light poured into the rooms, and Sunita drew the curtains.

Sunday is a lazy day, when the alarm clock need not be set. When Simran got up late, so did Sunita. By the time she had brushed, her maid was ready with a cup of tea which she placed on the table. She drank tea, and read the morning newspaper. Sunita was busy in the kitchen. If Praseetha Amma stayed overnight, both of them would have their breakfast together. Simran would take a quick bath and leave for her college.

A jar of mango pickles sat on a small stool. Praseetha Amma had brought it for Bunny. Simran intended to visit her son the coming weekend.

'Remind me to take this jar when I go to see Bunny,' she had told Sunita. The maid nodded. Sunita had also decided to pack delicious food for Bunny baba.

Once they were a happy family.

'I want to tell you about Swati,' she remembered Mr. Kaul telling her, 'she has married.'

He searched for interest on Simran's face. She showed no emotion. It did not matter to her.

'You can consider me your friend,' his words echoed, long after he had left, 'and trust me with any kind of information you wish to be conveyed to your husband.'

She nodded, and smiled at him.

'I have an appointment at six,' she had to say finally, when she saw Mr. Kaul intended to stay for sometime.

'Oh yes,' he had replied, 'can I drop you somewhere?'

Simran looked for Mary's address.

As they drove towards Mary's place, Mr. Kaul continued speaking. Simran hardly responded.

William opened the door. The hair on his chest peeped out of his T-shirt. He had grown his sideburns longer.

'Mary has gone to the shop to get us something to drink,' he smiled at her, taking her towards the living room.

'I have missed you terribly these past few months,' he said, looking into her eyes. 'I had tried to call you up several times. But you did not take my calls.'

Many a time Simran did not take calls thinking they were from her troublesome students.

She spoke with difficulty, her throat was parched.

As Mary entered the house, she smiled. Simran was sitting close to her brother.

'Tell her all about Marilyn,' the younger woman spoke as she poured drinks for all the three.

'We had liked each other a few years ago, but it is all over now,' William looked at Simran as he said.

'At least from my side', he added, after a while.

'So my brother is madly in love with you,' Mary smiled.

'How is everyone at Sothavilai?' Simran asked. 'I hope Matilda has recovered.'

'Yes, to a great extent. Though mother does not want her to go anywhere right now. She wants her to stay with her for a few more months.'

'How is Bunny?' Mary asked, stretching her legs on her table. 'I am sorry for this indecency,' she said, pointing towards her legs, 'but I find this very comfortable, especially at this stage.'

'It's all right,' both Simran and William said in unison.

William offered to drop Simran back. When they drove back, William held the steering with his right hand, and with his left hand, he held Simran. He kissed lightly. It was dark. Simran had a feeling William took a longer route intentionally. He stopped in a dark alley. There was dense vegetation on both sides. He unfastened his seat belt, and moved closer to her. Her heart throbbed as he started caressing her. She let out a low moan.

Their car stood in a corner.

'Marilyn often said I was not her William. She said my heart lay elsewhere.'

Simran wanted to ask hundreds of questions, but she did not. She was too happy with William. She saw her face in the mirror glow with a reddish tinge. It was quite late at night, but she was not bothered. She could have remained there the whole night.

She heard someone whisper. Someone seemed to be hiding amongst the thick vegetation. They drove on.

Simran took a flight next Monday. She reached her son's hostel early in the morning, as the boys trooped towards the college mess for their breakfast. Simran was in elements throughout her journey. Life was not that dreary, after all. A smile hovered on her lips as she remembered William.

Bunny waved at his mother and took quick steps towards her. He was carrying a mug of coffee in his hands.

'So mamma dear has found time for her son!' he smiled, as he walked closer to her.

'My friends are eager to meet you,' saying so, he suggested going to the mess with her. Simran agreed. She smiled as she saw all the boys stand in a row, with food on their plates. As Bunny introduced his mother to his friends, they touched her feet.

Bunny was growing up. Very soon he would finish his studies, and set up his own family. She remembered Varun as she looked at her son.

'Papa bought me this,' he showed her a P.C. that sat on his study table.

'When did he come over?' she asked.

'A week ago. He said he did not have matters for two-three days, so he decided to come here.'

'We had great fun when he came. We would roam around the whole day, eating in the restaurant when hungry. We carried bottles of Bisleri in the taxi and had great fun.'

'How did you get the permission for all this?'

'Papa can convince anyone, you know.'

Bunny loved his father.

'What about mamma?'

'Oh, she is a sweet darling.'

'Take a quick bath and get ready. I want to meet your hostel warden.'

The warden was a thin, balding man.

'Your son is doing well,' he said, throwing a kind look at Bunny, 'the only problem is, at times, he overstrains himself. I tell him, "Go easy son." But he does not listen to me. I am told both his parents have done quite well in life, academically.'

Simran smiled. Like mother, like son. She had also overstrained herself as a student. At times she wondered if it was all worth it. If she had stayed at home, cooked and cleaned, and remained a simple housewife, may be she would have led a more contented life.

She returned on Sunday, by the evening flight.

Mr. Kaul came again next evening. He came with a colleague.

'He practices in the Chennai High Court,' he introduced the lawyer to her.

Simran remembered going to Chennai High Court once, with Varun. Lawyers sat in the overcrowded verandah. Some walked fast, attending to matters.

Mr. Kaul's friend had a heavy accent.

'Why did you come to Chennai from Delhi?' he asked, clearing his throat.

'I like your beaches and nice, clean roads', she answered, with a smile.

'Delhi has better roads,' he answered. 'Of course, it has no sea.'

Praseetha Amma sat on the settee, cutting vegetables for the dinner. She stared at the two men every now and then.

'You are lawyers. Why don't you ask her husband to come and take her away with him?' she asked, looking at Mr. Kaul directly.

The two excused themselves after a while.

Praseetha Amma had arthritis, her fingers were all crooked. Yet, she attempted to help in the kitchen.

'My son wants me to join him,' Amma was telling Simran, 'and I am thinking seriously of accepting his proposal.'

'Amma, I will be the happiest if you go and stay with your son,' Simran said, looking at the old lady brightly. At times she pitied Amma, when she saw her fighting the diseases that are common at this age. She took care to bring the old lady to her place during those times, but she sincerely wished her son would take her with him.

She imagined herself twenty years from them, old and infirm.

Sunita lobbied with Praseetha Amma that they go back to Delhi.

'I overheard Kaul sahib say that Swati memsahib is married,' the maid was telling her, 'we will go back. We will ask Bunny baba to finish his studies and set up his practice in Delhi. We will live together.'

'And what will you do when Bunny baba gets married? Will you still tie him to your apron strings?'

One day as Simran sat in her balcony, she saw Praseetha Amma walk with a young man. Praseetha Amma looked up, and waved at her.

'My son!' Amma shouted from below. 'He came yesterday.'

Amma's son was fair, and had moustaches.

'He has given dharna here in my house,' Amma smiled, 'this time he is determined he will not go till his mother goes with him.'

Amma gave a toothless smile, and looked at her son fondly.

'Amma, you must go,' Simran shouted from her balcony. 'Sunita and I will come tomorrow and help you pack your bags.'

It was amusing to see Amma take out her things from her steel trunk. Her husband had brought her a set of red bangles with his first salary. Amma still had them. The shirt that her son had worn when he went to school for the first time formed part of her treasure. As Sunita helped the old woman empty the steel trunk and spread its contents on her bed, Amma had laughed. She cried too.

More than half a century of the woman's life lay packed and stored in that tiny steel trunk.

Her son had gone to the market to buy suitcases. He came back after an hour, and placed the large suitcases near the bed.

'Amma, please leave these here,' he cried exasperatedly, as he looked at her treasure.

'No way,' Amma was firm, 'if I go, these things go with me.'

'Shall I prepare tea for all of you?' Sunita rose.

'I will be most thankful,' the old woman's son said, as he flopped on the bed.

They sat on the bed, sipping tea. All were silent. Amma had become a part of them, and Simran knew Sunita and she would miss her. They would have been lonely in Chennai, but for her. Amma had made them feel at home.

'Amma, will you remember us when you are with your children?'

Amma looked at Sunita fondly. She touched her lightly on her shoulders and said, 'You two are like my children. How can I forget you?'

'Last month when I was on bed for almost a week, the two of them attended on me,' she was telling her son. 'Had they not been with me, I would not have been living today.'

They worked for the next few hours, chatting and packing. Amma was apprehensive about living abroad. But she had to go. Her home was where her son lived.

'We will have our dinner outside,' Amma's son announced. Sunita got up, her face and hands covered with dust. She got a wet piece of cloth and wiped dust off the suitcases. The rooms were in a mess, with newspapers and pieces of paper littered on the floor.

Sunita washed her face.

They drove off. They ate in a typical South Indian restaurant. The ladies had *masala dosa*. He had an onion *utthapam*.

'I miss these things abroad,' he said wistfully. 'But maybe Amma will cook for me. When Amma is with me, I will be a happier man.'

'Is your wife not taking good care of you?' Amma asked.

'She has a hectic schedule, Amma,' her son smiled. 'We have to manage with tinned and canned food most of the time.'

'Once I am there, things will change.' She looked determined. Simran knew there will be a major confrontation between the two women.

They were to leave the next day. Simran and Sunita came over to Praseetha Amma's place very early in the morning, and helped her pack up everything. Her son had talked to a broker and the house had been let out to a young couple. Amma had locked one room which she retained for herself.

'She will never leave Chennai,' her son laughed, as he saw Amma packing her things and locking them in the room. The tenants were to shift the next day.

When Amma's suitcases were loaded on the taxi, Sunita cried. So did Simran.

The old woman hugged them, and left.

21

She Refuses Him

Simran saw Swati on television. She was part of a panel of lawyers discussing 'Women Empowerment and Law.' She was being asked whether the law should be amended and death penalty be given for the offence of rape. Simran could not hear Swati's response. She increased the volume of the television. A male lawyer, also a part of the panel, was against the extreme punishment. By and large, they were in favour of capital punishment if the victim was a minor, or the act itself was such that it deserved such an extreme punishment.

The show went on for about half an hour. Swati is doing well, Simran thought, as she changed the channel. Varun had chosen well. She wondered if he still had a relationship with the young woman; going by Mr. Kaul's account, it was all over between them.

'I don't like Chennai without Praseetha Amma.' Sunita sat on the floor, near her mistress. She spoke again as she peeled potatoes, 'Amma also did not seem to be very happy leaving us. Did you see with what disinterest she sat in the taxi? I am certain she will not be happy there.'

Simran remembered what Amma said, before leaving, 'Go back to your husband. A woman is the happiest when she is with her family.'

Varun was a kind man, she knew. If she ignored his escapades, he was a thoughtful husband. And if he had strayed, so had she.

The other day she thought of her husband, who struggled to run the household in her absence. He had sent Sunita to his wife, and he managed with a part-time help. Simran was bored, and wanted a change. Not once did he object to her decision to shift to Chennai. It was a different matter that Varun took advantage of her absence. Yet, he could have neglected her. He came to Chennai, bought a house for her. He purchased everything needed for her comfort.

Bunny was fond of his father, and Sunita doted on her master.

If Varun had cheated her, so had William. William said he rang her up, but if he had really cared for Simran, he could have taken pains to trace her. He said he did not care for Marilyn any more. If that was true, why did he go to her, night after night? For a woman, sex and love go together.

Simran had sudden swings of mood. Sometimes the thought of William brought back pleasant memories. His commitment towards his family, the grit with which he had faced adversity, all this made her admire him.

Yet, at times he came across as a weak man.

Simran went to Marina Beach, after a long time. She was alone. Sunita remained at home, to wash clothes.

Simran put her feet in water, and watched the sun set. Curiously, the waves made a lot of noise. A woman, her legs exposed, had dipped them in water. She smiled at Simran. Her daughter played with water.

'Your children?' the woman asked casually.

'I have a son. He is in the hostel.'

'Grown up?' she asked.

Simran nodded.

'You are lucky. My daughter is very young. My days are spent in looking after her.'

'Yes,' Simran said. 'I think you are luckier,' she continued. 'Bringing up children has its own pleasures. When the child grows up, it is difficult to fill the void.'

Simran looked at the waves. They looked black, and dangerous.

'I think I must leave now,' she told the lady.

The child waved at her.

The dinner was light. Sunita was busy watching one of her favourite serials, a tearjerker. Simran carried her dinner to the living room and joined her.

Sunita switched off the television, wiping her tears. Simran smiled.

'Go and have your dinner,' she admonished her softly, 'you should not have it so late.'

Sunita sniffed, and went to the kitchen. She had a quick dinner, and then did the dishes. When she came to Simran's bedroom, she told her, 'Memsahib, there was a call from Sahib when you were away. He said he would leave for London in a week's time and will come back after a month. He wanted you to come over for a few days, before he left.'

Simran turned around, and looked at her maid.

'I will call him up tomorrow,' saying so she took a turn, and continued reading her novel. She was making a mental calculation of the number of days she had been on leave that year.

William came to her college. As she was leaving the Staff Room, she saw him stand in the corridor, with a bunch of red roses in his hands. Simran smiled. They went to a restaurant. It was lunch time, the place was abuzz with activity.

'I want you to come to Sothavilai with me,' he said.

'My mother wants to meet you,' he added.

'Is Mary coming?' she asked.

'She is in Sothavilai. With my mother around, it will be easier to take care of the baby.'

'Varun wanted me to come to Delhi for a few days. Maybe I can go to Sothavilai for a day, and then join Varun in Delhi.'

Simran shopped for Mary's child before she left for Sothavilai. She bought diapers, a small bath tub, baby clothes, and a rattle. Packing all this in her bag, she went with William.

They did not speak much on the way. Warm wind blew as they drove.

When they reached Sothavilai, they saw Mary stand on the steps, biting into an apple. Matilda came forward, a smile on her face.

William and Simran went to the beach in the evening. William was quiet. Simran stood, her hands on her hips. She could still see people getting tossed into sea, shrieking, getting carried away by waves.

Why did they have to come here to re-live what was extremely traumatic?

William took Simran to his friends, the fishermen. They were very polite, and wanted to know why she had not come to Sothavilai for so long.

'Chennai is a big city,' they smiled, 'Simran did not want to come to a small village.'

Simran was happy to see them laugh and smile.

'Why don't you go with us for fishing?'

'This time I have come for a day. Maybe next time,' she replied.

'If you stay here for a month, they will make an expert fisherwoman out of you.'

Matilda had cooked a delicious dinner for them. They chatted, as they sat and ate. All were concerned for Mary, who was not keeping well.

Simran got up in the morning and went to William's room. He was sitting, a towel wrapped around his torso.

'I want to know at what time we are leaving,' she said, as she saw William get up. He pulled her to his knees, and pressed his lips against hers. She gasped, and bit his cheeks. He smelt of after shave lotion. She clung to him for support.

Matilda entered the room. She stood there for a moment, her mouth wide open.

'Mother said you should take a *saree* she has bought, a small gift for you.' She looked directly at Simran as she spoke. Simran averted her eyes. William looked out of the window.

Matilda left the room immediately. William spoke after a while.

'Pack up. We will leave in an hour.'

They had a hurried breakfast. Simran ate, with her head bowed. When they were leaving, William's mother handed over a packet to her. Simran thanked her and left, with a promise to pay another visit soon.

They sat close to each other, as William drove back. On way, he stopped the car twice. Unfastening his seatbelt, he kissed her.

The journey back to Chennai was enjoyable. When the car pulled up before Simran's house, she got down. She clutched at her bag. She hummed a tune as she rang the doorbell.

Sunita looked worried as she opened the door.

'Was your mobile switched off? Sahib has been ringing up continuously. He said he wanted to talk to you urgently.'

Simran came inside, changed into a nightdress. She called up her husband.

'Bunny,' Varun's voice shook, 'fell down, and broke his bones. I am in the hospital with him.'

Simran did not know how to react. She could not speak.

She spoke with some difficulty.

'I will come as soon as I can.'

Sunita overheard her. Bunny baba was her precious darling too.

'I will go along with you, memsahib,' she implored.

Simran nodded.

After an hour she got a call from Varun.

'I am taking Bunny to Delhi,' he said, 'you reach there directly.'

Simran packed her suitcase with essential clothes, and some other things. Sunita had a tiny, red-coloured bag in which she kept her neatly folded *sarees*. She called a taxi and they reached the airport much before reporting time.

Her son's both legs were in plaster.

'Oh mamma!' he exclaimed, and smiled, as his mother came to him. 'And my dear Sunita is also here.' He extended his hand towards the maid, who stood in a corner.

Bunny's legs were propped on cushions.

'It is so cool,' he pointed towards his legs smilingly, 'I am taking complete rest, and all of you are here with me.'

Varun was in the kitchen, giving instructions to the part-time maid. Sunita came.

'You leave, sahib, both of us will manage.'

Varun smiled. The kitchen was Sunita's territory, and she could not tolerate any one prying into her area. He wondered if he would be able to retain the part-time maid. Sunita would make it difficult for her.

'Last time when you had met with an accident, your Papa had attended to you. I am sure he is a better nurse than I am.'

'I am happy with mamma and Papa around.'

Bunny looked happy. Despite the fact that both his legs were plastered, there was glow on his face.

'Won't you prepare something really delicious for your Bunny baba?'

'Anything for you,' the maid said, and ran to the kitchen. She came back with a tray loaded with onion *pakodas*, potato sandwiches, and sauce. She got a glass of water, and placed it at the corner of the tray. Simran helped Bunny get up, and both the women fawned over him.

'These two women will spoil me, Papa,' Bunny spoke, his mouth stuffed with food; he seemed to enjoy all the attention being paid to him, nonetheless.

After about an hour, Bunny went off to sleep. Simran decided to take a walk.

She did miss Delhi. She was born in Delhi, all her childhood memories were associated with the place.

She saw one of Bunny's childhood friends cycling past her. He stopped when he saw Simran. He folded his hands. He had secured admission in BITS, Pilani.

'What are you doing in Delhi?'

'Auntie, my grandfather had died. When I got a call from Papa, I came here immediately.'

Simran decided to pay a visit to his parents that day.

The colony was beautiful, with clean, tree-lined roads, and neat houses.

She went to meet Ms. Mishra in the evening. Her children were playing in the park. When they saw her, they ran to her.

'Mamma, Simran auntie is here,' they cried in unison.

Ms. Mishra was happy to see Simran.

'Oh God, I don't believe this,' she cried, 'now my Simran speaks with a South Indian accent.' And she started mimicking her.

'So you are doing well in Chennai!' Ms Mishra spoke after a while, with some seriousness. 'I read your political analyses and columns in newspapers and periodicals.'

'I have time to do it. Bunny has grown up.'

'I am told you have edited some books too.'

Simran nodded.

'Lucky woman,' Ms. Mishra looked at her wistfully, 'you have done well.'

They talked of their college, and the teachers.

'Ms. Singh has started looking old. She forgets things easily. Her world revolves around Cookie.'

Simran decided to pay her a visit on the morrow. She wanted to talk to the old lady.

At night, as Simran lay next to her son, Bunny snuggled close to her.

'Ma, I had wanted to tell you something,' he said, coming to her closer.

She looked at him.

'I want to go to England for my further studies. I hope you do not have any objections to it.'

'Why should I have, my son?'

'Ma, I intend to settle there.'

Simran did not speak for a while.

'Papa has promised to take me to England when he goes there. I will make enquiries.'

They talked in whispers, till late at night. Simran did not know when she went off to sleep.

Ms. Singh was not at home when Simran went to see her. Brigadier Singh was at home, sitting on the verandah, tying his turban.

He welcomed her warmly, giving her a big hug.

'Ms. Singh will be back in a moment,' he said, while offering her a glass of water. 'She has gone to fetch milk from the dairy.'

Brigadier Singh continued tying his turban, as he spoke to her. 'My wife could not live without Cookie, and she brought her back.'

'When are you coming back?'

Simran was taken aback. She did not expect Singh Saab would ask the question so pointedly.

Ms Singh came back, a look of tiredness on her face. Her face glowed with warmth as she saw Simran, sitting in her living room.

'What a pleasant surprise!' she squeaked, as she opened the refrigerator and placed the packet of milk inside.

They talked of old times.

'The faculty is not the same without you.'

'But you are doing well,' Ms. Singh added.

Simran enquired about Cookie. 'Oh, she has gone to her parents. They had taken a short vacation, and have taken Cookie along with them.'

When she came back home, her son was sleeping. He woke up, as he heard soft footsteps of his mother.

'Mamma, you haven't told me as yet. Shall I go with Papa and find out about the courses?'

'Yes. But make sure you get a good university. You need not go abroad just for the sake of it.'

Bunny hugged his mother.

'Are you sure you will recover by then?'

'Papa has decided to postpone his trip. He has promised to extend it by a month.'

By then, Bunny's legs would heal, she expected.

'So Mamma is having a great time, meeting her friends,' Bunny wrapped his hands around Simran, and came closer to her.

'I am surprised, but Ms. Singh looks old,' she said, still not recovering from the fact that someone as beautiful as Ms. Singh could look old and haggard.

'What about Mishra auntie?'

'Oh, she is as vivacious as ever,' she smiled. 'She claims I have acquired a South Indian accent, and was trying to mimic me.'

Bunny guffawed.

'But these ladies love you. Papa tells me they keep asking about you.'

'Mamma, Swati auntie has married. Papa told me there is nothing between them.'

Simran tried smiling, running a finger in her son's hair. Now that Swati had left him, Varun wanted her back. He was trying to seek the help of her son, her friends.

They had mutton biryani for dinner. Food was ordered from outside. Sunita cut thin onion rings. She laid the table. The bowl of biryani was at the centre, with onion rings and green chutney.

They watched television as they ate.

Swati was on television, discussing the proposed legislation that sought to make judiciary more accountable. The panel included a minister from the ruling party, an important BJP man, and a few lawyers.

Varun looked at Simran. She watched television, listening to the discussion with attention.

'I want more,' Bunny shouted from his room, and Sunita ran to replenish his plate.

Swati had a husky voice, and she thought before she spoke. There was a verbal duel between men from both the parties. It was a sensitive topic, and the coordinator was trying to cool down tempers. They discussed judicial activism.

Swati said that the tussle between the Legislature and the Judiciary had existed right since independence, and attempted to trace its history.

'Neither is superior,' she emphasized, chewing every word, 'it is the constitution that is sovereign, and all must look to it for power, and remain within their limit.'

Varun smiled.

Post dinner, they sat with Bunny.

'It is not fair,' he was cribbing. 'Papa did not pack any of my books while coming to Delhi. I am missing so much. I cannot even read my books.'

'I have brought you straight from the hospital. And how would I know which books to pack?'

'We will play carom,' Simran suggested. None was in a mood to sleep. They carried the board to Bunny's bed, and started playing, their eyes chasing the striker. Bunny and Sunita were partners, Simran teamed up with Varun. Bunny was a good player, his parents lost both the games to him. They had coffee after one game was over. Bunny looked cheerful, victory had made him buoyant.

'Bunny baba, we have won the first game. We should win the second one too.'

There was a glint in Bunny's eyes. He struck with vengeance, winning the second round within ten minutes.

No one likes defeat. But defeat at the hands of an offspring is most welcome.

At night, Varun embraced his wife. He ran his fingers in her hair. He could see Simran was greying rapidly.

After a while, he spoke, 'Come back, Simran.'

Simran remained silent for the next five minutes. She had buried her face in the pillow, her hair spreading out. Then she got up, and drank water from a chilled bottle; droplets of water ran down her chest. Despite it being cold, she felt she was perspiring. She looked at Varun. He was naked, and perspired profusely. This man had loved her once, passionately. And then he had cheated her.

Did she want to come back?

Varun moved closer to his wife, touching her lightly on her cheeks.

'Please,' he said, looking at her with hope.

'I like Chennai,' she said finally, 'and I am going back.'

She packed off, and left. Her heart ached as she took leave of Bunny.

William rang her up informing her that Mary had given birth to a baby girl. He had come to visit Simran after coming back from Sothavilai.

'Marilyn has not been keeping well,' he spoke with concern, 'I think I will have to give more time to her.'

Simran said nothing. She had never objected to his going to Marilyn.

In fact, she felt she needed no one. After the initial sense of dread and insecurity was over, she felt much more relaxed.

She went to Sothavilai for a day to see Mary's daughter. Mary looked harassed. The child was very weak. She slept through the day and kept awake at night. Mary had to remain awake throughout night, giving feed to the child after every three hours. Thankfully she had her mother and sister who took care of the baby when she was tired. Single handedly, it would have been very difficult.

Bunny called up from the airport, as he was about to leave for England. He sounded happy.

One day as she was about to leave for college, she got a message on her mobile from her brother Sanjiv. He was also asking Simran to join Varun.

'You are my sister,' Sanjiv's voice cackled on the other side, 'I would never goad you into doing anything that is not good for you.'

Simran refused him.

'What will happen to you when you are old?' her brother persisted, 'you will need your husband.'

'If Varun wanted me so much, why did he not stop me when I had decided to teach in Chennai?'

Sanjiv said quietly, 'Forget all that, he wants to come back to you.'

Simran changed the topic.

Simran thought of her dead sister. She had cried bitterly, as her dead body was fished out of the sea. Simran had shaken her vigorously, searching for trace of life. When the fishermen had said, 'Take her back, and let her rest in peace,' she howled at the sea. When the fishermen surrounded her, consoling her, urging her to go back to the hotel and inform her parents, she felt she had grown up suddenly.

She had survived the tragedy. For many years, she cried as she remembered her sister howl and ask for help, as she stood and watched helplessly. Her voice rang in her ears.

And then her dead sister started fading from her memory. The pain subsided, and it did not hurt her any more.

The more she tried to cling to a man, the more she felt she was losing.

She envied those who had received unalloyed, pure love.

William had said he wanted to meet her in the evening. She had gone. She wondered why the face of her dead sister floated before her every time she went through trauma.

When she lived, her sister had been a great optimist. If you lose a leg, it is alright. You still have the other.

William looked at her intently, as he saw her lost in thoughts.

'How is Marilyn?' she enquired, after a while.

'She is fine. The children give her a tough time, but she knows how to manage them.'

Simran wore a beautiful emerald ring. Her hair was parted in the middle. She wore a black *saree*, bordered in gold, with silver sequins. She wore a heavy necklace, and a few bangles. William had looked at her admiringly, as she sat, cutting a striking figure.

'I have told Marilyn about our relationship,' he said after a while.

'She understands,' he continued. "Go ahead," she had said. "It is your life."

William ordered orange juice. A couple sat near their table. They were newly wed. They sat, peeping into each other's eyes.

'Does your husband know about us?'

She did not know, and she was not bothered.

William spoke a lot. He was in a cheerful mood. Simran merely nodded, responding in monosyllables.

'What happened? You seem to be lost somewhere.'

'Oh, it is nothing,' she smiled feebly. Her thoughts were elsewhere.

'I have got a beautiful gift for you,' he said.

Simran looked at him enquiringly.

William was smiling. 'I have talked to Marilyn and my mother. They have all accepted the fact that we cannot live without each other. And I have told them,' he added, 'that Simran and I will live together.'

'You did not consult me before you made this announcement', she looked at William pointedly.

'But Simran,' William pulled his chair closer to hers, 'you told me after you were back from Delhi that you do not intend to go back to your husband!'

'Yes, I did say so,' she was desperately trying to control her emotions.

So he was coming to her now. After going to Marilyn night after night!

'Didn't you expect to join me, after you had left your husband?'

She laughed softly.

'Where did you get such an idea from? I am happy the way I am, leading a carefree life.'

'Are you sure?'

'Yes, I am.'

William looked shocked. He had not expected this from her.

They left after a while.

'William,' she said as he dropped her, and was walking towards his car, 'Give me a break.' William stopped, colour drained from his face.

She went to her living room, and started going through the old photographs.

She found her little sister, smiling at her.

22

Why?

When Mary opened the door, she saw William. He entered his room silently and bolted the door from inside. He sat on a chair, and looked at the bare wall. The wall clock ticked, breaking the silence. He could hear Mary and her husband fight in the other room. The child cried, and they stopped shouting.

As a teenager, he had often imagined himself with Marilyn. He felt proud as he saw himself at her side. Marilyn was sweet and petite, and he would have been proud to wed her.

Marilyn went away. William felt something snap within. He had walked kilometres, listlessly, trying to erase her face from his memory. He had gone to his friends, sitting with them till late at night. He had lost interest in living. He would turn on the tap, and forget to turn it off.

Marilyn had also loved him. She rang him up from the US, at times. She cried, telling him she could not forget him. At times he banged his head against the wall in desperation. Many a time he had an impulse to fly to her; but when he looked at his widowed mother and sisters, he was reminded of his duty towards them. Marilyn was his first love, she gave him immense pain.

By and by, Marilyn's calls became less frequent. One day William heard that Marilyn had married an American. Both worked in the same organization. William sat on his bed, holding his head with both his hands. It took sometime to register that Marilyn whom he had often perceived as his wife, was now someone else's.

He had gone to the church and prayed silently. Jesus Christ looked down at him, both hands outstretched. An old man sat beside him. He looked at William, a strange expression on his face. He asked nothing. He waited for William to get up, and followed him out of the church. The old man made no attempt to talk to him.

One day he told him, 'My wife died a month back. She loved Jesus.'

After a few days, William stopped going to the church. But he often thought of the old man afterwards.

He married off Matilda. Marilyn divorced the American, and married a Hindu, settled in the US. He listened with composure. And then he fell ill. I would be happy if I die, he thought once. My responsibilities are over. Matilda and Mary would take care of Agnes.

He had recovered.

Simran entered his life. His heart throbbed every time he looked at her. Simran and Marilyn were so different! Simran was tall, with a stately figure; Marilyn was short and sweet.

William had a feeling Simran was attracted towards him. Every time he made a move, she reciprocated. He often stared at her. Simran, at those times, looked back, showing interest in him. She was like a whiff of fresh air. Simran was in Sothavilai for a few days; he remained at home most of the time, searching for an opportunity to be near her.

When the waves came crashing and Simran shrieked, he ran to save her. His faculties were numbed as he pulled her to a tree, saving her from drowning. He shed all inhibitions when he saw Death all around him.

Just when he had thought life was treating him kindly, he received a jolt. Agnes died. Matilda lost her baby. He staggered, looked for support, and found none. God had ordained him to experience pain.

Mary wanted to marry a Hindu she had met in Chennai. He had consented to it. It was her life, he did not want to interfere. They were happy, and he thanked God. He had made arrangements for the wedding. Mary's husband came from a respectable family. He saw to it that Hindu rites of marriage were performed, and then the marriage took place a second time in the Church. He forgot all his sorrows as he saw the happy faces of the couple.

He remembered Simran and wanted to contact her desperately. But he was frightened. Simran was a married woman, with a child. Her husband was a well-to-do lawyer. William could not match up to Varun. And he was certain, Simran who had shown momentary interest in him would have forgotten him. He wanted to run to Delhi, and take Simran in his arms. But when he thought of her staring at him coldly, refusing to recognize him, he had shuddered. He could take no more, he had had enough.

Once or twice he could not resist the temptation to talk to her. He called her up; Simran did not receive it. He stopped calling. He was certain Simran was not interested in him. When he went to Mary, he wanted to hear about Simran from his sister. But Mary had been newly married, and was soon in the family way. She was preoccupied; she did not have time to think beyond her baby. William looked at her wistfully as she blabbered. Not once did she refer to her ex-roommate. It was a short association that she chose to forget conveniently.

Life has its twists and turns. Marilyn who had left him and married twice, had come to Chennai. She was now a divorced woman, with three children. Marilyn wanted him back.

William was not interested in Marilyn any longer. She did not excite his passion the way Simran had done.

But she was determined to get William back. She was happy to learn that William was still unattached. Two men had shared their lives with her, and now that she looked back, she felt that she should not have left William.

William went to her. Every day, without fail. If he missed a single day, Marilyn got restless. She rang him up. 'Please come over,' she would plead. He was in Chennai quite often. But his relationship with Marilyn underwent a sea change. The spark that existed earlier was missing.

Simran was his love. She had given him succour. When he felt low in life, the thought of Simran had urged him to live. His heart skipped a beat when Mary mentioned Simran's name. He felt joyous as he learnt that she was still in Chennai. He was desperate to see her, and requested his sister to arrange for a meeting.

He saw Simran, looking as beautiful as ever. My darling, he whispered, as he looked at her. But Simran looked at him strangely. Though she never expressed her feelings openly, he knew she bore grudge against him. He wanted to tell her all about Marilyn, but she never questioned him.

Marilyn had asked hundreds of questions about Simran, and he had answered each one of them. He had bared his heart before her. Marilyn understood. William was no longer hers. And she would let him go.

But Simran asked no questions. How could he explain things to her unless she asked? He had an answer, only if Simran would question. Simran looked at him vacantly, her large eyes fixed on him. William did not know how to react. He would embrace her, trying to comfort her. Simran would pull herself away, resenting his touch.

Mary said Simran loved him, and felt she had been cheated.

In Sothvilai, Matilda stayed with her mother. Soon Mary joined them. Matilda forgot her sorrow and spent her days looking after Mary's child - a bonnie baby with soft, curly hair. She dressed up her sister's child in clothes she had stitched for her baby. She had knitted a baby pink sweater, with socks and caps, and every time the child wore the set, her eyes were moist with tears.

Mary took Matilda to a competent doctor in Chennai. Please do something, she had pleaded. Let my sister have a child of her own. The doctor had sounded helpless. Instead, she had given the address of an orphanage, and suggested Matilda adopt a child.

'I have known many couples who have adopted children, and are happy with their decision,' the doctor said. 'In fact,' she laughed, 'after a few years when the same couple came to me with their adopted child, I had a feeling the child started resembling the adoptive parents physically.' The doctor also gave the name of a social worker, unmarried, who was based in Chennai. The sole mission of the social worker's life was to provide for the orphaned children she brought up as her own.

William took Matilda to the social worker's place. The lady was middle-aged, her hair was greying, and she wore a crisp cotton *saree.* 'Even when we did not have enough to eat,' she smiled as she looked at Matilda, 'my parents never hesitated in helping others.'

Matilda had decided. She would adopt a child.

William was happy for her. Mary was back in Chennai. Their mother accompanied Mary. Mary's mother-in-law stayed with them. The two matrons struck a good friendship. They slept together, on the same bed. Both had seen life, and had much to say to one another. Mary's mother gifted a small idol of Natraj to her mother-in-law. Mary's mother-in-law was touched.

They took turns massaging the child, and feeding him. At times, when William was staying with them, he took the child on a pram and went for a walk.

The child loved it, and welcomed Uncle William with a smile every time he came near him. Sometimes William took the child to Simran. 'Mary's daughter,' Sunita would shout, and snatch the baby from William. She would squat on the floor, as the child lay on her lap, and talked to her endlessly. At times she took her to their garden, and showed her flowers. The child was attracted to bright flowers, and often tried plucking them. Simran and William would soon come after them. They would sit on the swing, and watch with a smile. Sunita ran around. At times Simran held the baby, and smiled. The baby gave her a smile.

William's mother knew her son had a soft corner for Simran. She saw him going through her political analyses, published in newspapers of Chennai. William read and re-read the same articles. She knew Simran had a special place in her son's life. Mary had also told her certain things. She was waiting for William to tell her about Simran.

One day, when Mary and the two matrons sat in the garden, Marilyn came. She had brought along with her her youngest child.

'Mary and William are inside,' their mother said.

Marilyn went inside. Her child played with Mary's daughter. William was reading, the newspaper covering his face. He had placed his legs on the table and was in a half-sitting position. Small cushions, with green and yellow boxes on the cover, were scattered around. On the side table stood the statue of Lord Buddha.

Marilyn sat next to William. William looked up, and smiled. He was reading an article by Simran, 'The *sanyasin* and the BJP.' Marilyn took the newspaper and saw William had underlined certain portions.

'The firebrand leader was removed from her post as the chief minister of Madhya Pradesh on a small pretext,' she read the highlighted portion. 'BJP has erred in removing a leader of such calibre, especially one who belonged to the grass root level.'

'Simran is quite an active lady,' she observed, as William folded the newspaper and placed it on the side table. 'I often see her walk past my house, taking long strides.' William nodded. Simran walked fast, he had seen.

Mary came with tea things. She set them on the table. As she sat, preparing tea, she threw an appreciative look at the newspaper. She had read the article in the morning.

'I agree with Simran,' she said.

William nodded.

'Where are your children?' Mary asked Marilyn, looking at her.

'Two have gone for their tuition, and the third has come with me.'

'Marilyn, don't your ex-husbands do anything for their children?' Mary asked.

'No,' Marilyn replied. 'I have never asked them for help.'

'I have a house of my own and a decent job. I need not worry.'

Mary sipped tea noisily. Her mother-in-law came inside, holding her baby.

'She is hungry,' she said, 'I think you should feed her.'

Mary went to her room to feed her child.

Marilyn kept talking for a long time. William replied in monosyllables. He was lost in his own thoughts.

'Remember to come tonight,' Marilyn whispered, as she rose. William wanted to say no, he did not want to go. He was missing Simran terribly, and could think of none else.

'Are you listening to me?' Marilyn nudged at him.

'I may be a bit late today,' he said, looking at Marilyn's eager face.

'I will wait for you', she said, as she picked up her purse and held her child's finger. 'Do not disappoint me.'

William was missing Simran terribly that day. When he could think of nothing else to do, he spread the newspaper article written by her. He read it once again. He felt Simran sat beside him, and talked to him. With a heavy heart he folded the newspaper and rose.

He took a quick shower and went for a walk. He felt he was at the crossroads. He had to make a choice.

That night William did not go to Marilyn.

He went to the seashore instead.

He had started meeting Simran regularly. Once she told him, as he was parking his car, 'My son intends to go to England for his further studies. He wants to settle there.'

He listened to her with interest. Often when he thought of his relationship with Simran, somehow her son had always been in the picture. Simran was quite attached to her son.

Varun had asked her to come back, she had said further. William looked at her, absorbing every word.

'I said I love Chennai,' she smiled faintly as she said. 'I am going back.'

William rose, dusting grains of sand. The waves were making a lot of noise. He looked at sea, endless.

'How will Varun manage?' he had asked, still not certain whether she was ready to leave Varun for him. What did he have to offer? Her husband was a successful lawyer and could provide all the comforts of life to her. She was erudite and successful.

Marilyn waited for him. He was not bothered. He had waited for her too long. She did not come back to him. She married twice, and decided to come back to India only after her marriages had failed.

As the clock struck twelve, Marilyn knew William would not come. Her children were asleep. She was sitting in her verandah alone, a solitary figure. She did not blame him. She sat examining the pearl ring, set in gold, adorning her finger. Another one, with two rows of diamond, was in her next finger. She was fond of jewellery, and loved wearing them.

In the last one hour, she drank two mugs of coffee. She sat and deleted all the messages on her mobile. When it was twelve and William did not come, she rose. She locked the main gate, and switched off the lights. She went inside, and slept.

William rang the doorbell at Mary's place. It was one in the morning. Except for Mary, all had gone off to sleep. Mary's child was awake, and crying. Mary was washing the bottles and filling them with lukewarm water and milk powder.

William held the baby, as Mary prepared the child's feed. The child became quiet and looked at Uncle William with interest.

Mary came with the bottle. William handed over the baby to her. The child had the milk noisily.

'Marilyn had called up an hour ago,' Mary said, looking at the child as he held the bottle with both his hands.

William said nothing in response. He knew Marilyn would have waited for him.

A few days later he went to Simran, in the evening. Sunita was dusting the crystals with a piece of cloth, and placing them carefully on the table. The flowers in the pots were in full bloom. Sunita carried two pots, with large yellow flowers, to the living room. The place shone. Her hands on her hips, Sunita looked around with satisfaction.

Simran was not at home. She had gone to attend a seminar. It was late at night when she came back, tired. She slumped on her sofa. Simran smiled as she saw William.

'Why do you overstrain yourself?' he questioned, as Simran reclined on the sofa, her eyes shut.

'You will kill yourself by overworking.'

'Who is bothered?'

William stayed for another hour. Then he left.

Sunita had a guest that night. A young boy, fourteen-fifteen years of age, stood at the entrance, as she was bolting the door. There was a striking resemblance between them.

'I am Gorakh,' the boy touched her feet.

Sunita glowed with happiness as she recognized her brother.

'My brother,' she introduced Gorakh to her mistress. He bowed to touch Simran's feet. Simran blessed him.

'The condition is not good in our village,' the boy was telling his sister. 'I was asked to come to you in search of a job.'

'Where do I get a job for you?' Simran was bewildered.

Simran sought William's help.

'Is he educated?' William asked.

'He has studied till class four.'

'Mary is in search of a domestic help. Let me talk to her.'

Mary came over. She talked to Simran and said she was willing to employ Gorakh.

'He can run errands for me. He can also help me in taking care of the child.'

'He is Sunita's brother. I am sure he will be as useful as his sister is.' Sunita gave an anxious look as her brother went away with Mary.

William stayed back. He stared at the charging bull, embroidered and hung in Simran's bedroom. Simran sat beside him, silently painting her nails.

'Marilyn seems to be quite harassed. Her children give her a tough time.'

William nodded.

'Yesterday as Marilyn was buying the vegetables, she fell. The vegetables were scattered on the road. Sunita was also there, she helped her in collecting them.'

William felt bad for Marilyn.

'The vegetable vendor sells vegetables right in front of her house,' Simran continued. 'Her eldest daughter ran to help her out. Marilyn went away, limping, supported by her daughter. Sunita was carrying her bag of vegetables.'

'She is an unfortunate woman,' William spoke, thinking of Marilyn, sprawled on the road, her vegetables scattered all over.

Simran threw a sharp look at him.

'I have to buy some textbooks. Tomorrow when I come back from the college, I will go to the bookshop.'

'I will take you to a very good bookshop. When do you intend to go?' William was eager to help.

'Are you free tomorrow, in the evening?'

'Yes.'

'Take me along with you,' Sunita butted in. 'You can drop me at Mary's place and collect me while returning.'

'I hope Gorakh has adjusted. I am concerned for him.'

'Oh, don't bother,' William said. 'He loves Mary's baby and seems to be quite happy there.'

'It has been three months since Bunny went to England,' Simran was saying as she drove towards the bookstore with William. 'He intends to come to Chennai for a week.'

Simran's face glowed as she mentioned her son's name.

'Why does Bunny want to settle abroad?' William asked, applying brakes.

Simran was silent. She had never thought on those lines.

They reached the bookstore. Simran started flipping through the pages of a hard bound book. It had a white cover, with the name of the author written in blue. As she moved slowly, examining books, her thoughts frequently went back to her son. Why did he want to settle abroad? Was it his ambition or something else that compelled him to leave India?

'They make me work very hard,' he had written. 'I am supposed to complete two years' course in one year.'

Bunny had enrolled himself in a prestigious university. The fee was high. Simran wondered how much Varun had paid for his admission. He never discussed finances with her.

She selected four books and brought them to the counter. As she unzipped her purse, her mobile fell down. The sim card got detached. The man at the counter was busy. After about five minutes, he attended to Simran. She handed over her credit card, to make the payment.

William bought some books on fiction. They went to a restaurant for coffee. They sipped coffee, as William talked of his fishermen friends.

'They always talk about you.'

'How is Matilda?'

'She has gone back to her husband. She dotes on the child she has adopted.'

Simran wondered if one felt the same kind of attachment towards an adopted child. The fact of adoption made no difference, she was told, and many a time the adopted child gave more pleasure.

Mary's house was in a mess. Her child was in a bad mood, and they had a tough time. Gorakh was cutting vegetables, his hands moving up and down on the chopping board. Sunita was watering the plants in the garden, talking to Mary's mother-in-law all the while.

'Your brother does not listen to me at times,' she was cribbing.

'Scold him if he does so,' Sunita threw an angry look towards the kitchen.

'With his belly full, he has started throwing tantrums,' she muttered, cursing Gorakh.

William blew the horn. Simran and Sunita rushed towards his car.

When they reached home, Sunita asked William to stay back for dinner.

They had chapattis with curry. Sunita brought strawberry custard in two small bowls. She went to make bed for Simran.

Marilyn called up William, on his mobile. His phone was on vibration mode. He received her call, as he saw Marilyn's name being displayed.

'I miss you,' she sounded sad as she spoke. William threw a glance at Simran. Simran had told him she intended to stay back in Chennai permanently. He was also aware of Bunny's plans.

Simran loved him, he was certain. She had left Varun for him, he thought as he said good night to her. He intended to see Marilyn on the way.

Marilyn sat on an armchair as William entered her living room. Her eldest child was pressing her head. She ran inside to get juice for William.

'My first husband has written this.' She gave a short laugh as she spoke.

'He is marrying again and I have been invited to attend his wedding.'

'Is he marrying an American?'

'I don't know.'

William read the letter as Marilyn helped her daughter with the homework. Her bracelet shone as she sat, correcting her child's work.

The child went away, taking the school bag with her.

'Wash your face before you go to sleep,' Marilyn shouted, 'and apply some night cream.'

The child said something in response which William could not hear.

'So you are coming from Simran's house!' she gave a penetrating look.

'Yes.'

'She will not go back to Delhi.'

'No. She will not.'

'I think something in Chennai holds her back. Is that you?'

'Marilyn' William spoke finally, after a short pause. 'I am immensely fond of Simran and I intend to live with her.'

'I knew,' Marilyn said. 'I wish you all the best. I wish you are luckier than me in your relationship,' she said, with a smile.

He spoke to Simran.

Simran refused him.

23

The Son Goes

Simran peeled off an orange. She ate, looking at the flowers that grew in clumps. Some of the plants were supported by sticks, tied to them. She sat serenely, doing nothing in particular. Sunita too sat silently, looking at the rows of pots. Both thought of Bunny, who was to come to Chennai for a week.

'Monica Lewinsky has taken admission along with me,' Bunny's eyes twinkled as he wheeled out his bags. Simran had come to receive him.

Sunita sprang to her feet as they rang the bell. Bunny talked for the next two hours. He had a lot to say. Sunita rose after a while, and emerged with a large mug of milk and Bournvita.

'Give me some coffee,' Bunny showed mock anger, pecking Sunita on her cheeks.

Sunita looked at Simran for support.

Simran laughed.

'He is a man now, dear,' she said. 'Let him have his coffee.'

'When he was with me, he had his glass of milk regularly.' Sunita went away, muttering, and looked for the gas lighter.

Bunny opened a jar and had biscuits. 'Life is very hectic, Ma,' he was saying, as he discussed his days' routine with his mother. 'By the time I am on my bed, I am very tired.'

'Have you made any girl friend there?' Simran smiled, looking at her son mischievously.

Bunny made a face. He placed the empty mug on the table and went to the washroom. He came back, and was sprawled on the sofa.

'Ma, take out my shoes.' He felt like a king, being attended to by two women. He then asked Sunita to get his bag. He had purchased some gems for his mother. There were gifts for Sunita too.

'These are expensive gifts.' Simran looked at her son with suspicion. 'Where did you get the money from?'

'Papa sends me more than enough.' He looked at his mother fondly. 'He calls me up regularly and sends me more than I ask for.'

Varun was a large-hearted father. Simran knew.

'Bunny,' Simran asked suddenly, 'do you remember promising the villagers of Sothavilai that you will work for them? Why don't you come back to India?'

'I want to explore the world.' His voice held the calmness of the sea, after the storm. 'And India holds no charm for me since Papa and you have started living separately.'

'Both your parents are ready to lay their lives for you, son!' Her heart ached as she saw her son's face.

Bunny went to Delhi for two days. Delhi was under a spell of cold wave and Simran had ensured he was covered from head to toe when he was there.

Varun beamed, as he went to the airport to receive him.

He took his son to a shopping mall and bought him a leather coat. They drove on the roads of Delhi aimlessly. Traffic in South Delhi moved slowly.

'I have a conference at twelve-thirty,' Varun told his son, as he pulled before another Mall. 'Shop to your heart's content. I will come back right after the conference is over. If there is any problem, I am available on my mobile.' Varun gave a smile to his son as he drove off.

The conference went on for a long time. The counsel he was briefing was over-worked. But he was sharp and dedicated. As Varun showed the relevant pages, he scribbled on the blank sheet attached to the brief.

'Do some research on this,' the counsel said, as he marked a few lines with a highlighter. 'I want to know what the Apex Court has held earlier on this.' Varun thought of his junior, Atishi. He hoped he had access to SCC online. I will call him to the office for a few hours today, he decided as he gathered his papers, and thanked the counsel. For a few seconds, he thought of Swati. Had she been working in his office, she would have managed to search for a case law, pat on the point. He could depend on Swati. He was not so sure about Atishi.

Bunny rang up. 'When are you coming, Papa? I am tired of shopping. I want to go home.'

'You come to the parking,' Varun replied, walking hurriedly towards his car. 'I will reach within ten minutes.' He cursed as the lights turned red. Bunny planned to go back to Chennai next evening. And three days later, he was scheduled to fly back to England.

Bunny saw Varun had left Simran's clothes in the cupboard. Her *sarees* still hung in a row. Simran had not bothered to take them to Chennai, and Varun had not displaced them. Bunny felt his mother still lived in the house.

'Ma looked regal when she wore this.' He pointed towards a *chanderi saree* that hung in a corner.

'Your Ma looks regal in anything she wears.'

'Then what went wrong between you, Papa?'

Varun looked at his son. Bunny had questioned his father for the first time.

'Your Ma does not forgive easily, 'Varun replied.

Bunny knew. He had seen his parents fight, and Varun had to go on his knees before Simran relented. He felt sympathetic towards his father.

Back in Chennai, Simran and her maid had spent the entire day cooking for Bunny. When Bunny came, he threw the bag and sprang towards the plate of fish. Simran laughed.

'Wash your hands. All this is for you.'

'I am starved,' Bunny spoke, as he bit into the fish.

After dinner, they watched television. Bunny went to sleep early. He was tired.

Simran sat in her study and began writing. She had started contributing articles to the newspapers more regularly.

Sunita sat at her feet as she wrote. She went to sleep only after her mistress did.

'It is late' Simran shot an angry look at her. 'Go to bed.'

'What about you? Shall I allow you to kill yourself by over-working?'

'Sunita, writing for a few extra hours does not kill anybody.' The mistress smiled as she gave a fond look to Sunita.

Sunita got up slowly and started making the bed.

'Change the All-Out Refill, the mosquitoes are biting me.' Sunita opened the drawer and took out a fresh refill.

There was complete silence for the next one hour. Finally Simran rose, and went to the washroom. She came back and switched off the lights. Simran smiled as she heard Bunny snore in the other room.

Simran went to attend her classes the next day. Sunita went to the grocer.

'Have your tea, baba.' She placed the hot cup of tea on the side table. 'I will be back in half an hour.'

Bunny yawned, and opened his eyes.

'I'll shut the door,' he stared out of the window, clutching at his sheet.

He shut the door and came back to his room. As he drank his tea, he flipped through the pages of *Femina*, the women's magazine. He had picked it up from his mother's room. An exceedingly attractive woman, her body half-exposed, stared back at him. They had carried the article, 'Bra weaver's guide to a great bust.' Bunny's hands reached his groins.

There was sex info in the inside pages. The sexologist gave tips on intercourse and satisfaction during sex.

Sunita came back soon afterwards, her hands clutching the big shopping bags.

'Get me another cup of tea.' Bunny stretched himself, and looked at Sunita drowsily.

'I will get you a glass of milk.' The maid threw a stern look at Bunny.

Sunita got the glass of milk. Bunny spilled its content in the wash basin.

'Now you can get me tea,' he smiled. Did Sunita think he was in kindergarten?

As Sunita got busy doing the daily chores, he decided to go out for a walk. He remembered Varun's face. Papa has been a dutiful guardian. He deserves another chance. Bunny plucked a leaf as he walked. He reached the Marina Beach. The waves beckoned him. He sat, dipping his feet in seawater. He watched with curiosity as the sea ebbed. Marriage was not so sacrosanct in the West, he had seen. In fact, he smiled as he remembered his classmates taking leave to attend their fathers' wedding. It was different in India. Marriage was still considered a sacred institution, and its annulment a source of great pain.

Since childhood he had heard his father say he loved his mother. What went wrong? He had not stopped loving anyone of them. And why was Ma so stubborn?

Simran was back when Bunny came back in the evening. She was exhausted. They rested for an hour or two. Simran did not know why she felt so restless.

'I have a lot of work today,' she looked at her son. 'I will take late dinner. Do not wait for me.'

Sunita looked at her mistress. She knew Simran would go to her room and drink.

'Baba, you eat and go off to sleep.' Sunita laid the table, pulling a chair for Bunny. Bunny knew his mother worked and drank in her study.

'Does Ma drink frequently?'

'No. But when she is upset, she does.'

'Is she always upset?'

'No baba.' Sunita heaped two scoops of ice cream in a bowl.

'Your mother has swings of mood. Sometimes she is very cheerful,' the maid continued, 'at other times she is a picture of pathos, looking out of the window listlessly for hours. At times I have seen her cry, but she keeps herself busy most of the time.'

Bunny went to Praseetha Amma's house with Sunita. The tenant took care of the place. Big cauliflowers and cabbages could be seen everywhere. The flowers looked bright in sunshine.

'Praseetha Amma is coming for a week.' Sunita informed Mr. Wilson, the tenant. 'I have come to clean the room for her.'

As Sunita took the keys, Bunny went for a stroll in the garden. Sylvia, Mr. Wilson's wife, was watering the cauliflowers. Her daughters were busy tending to the flowers.

Bunny struck a conversation with Sylvia. The latter was an unfortunate woman Her only son had died after prolonged illness. She had left her place and had come to Chennai soon thereafter.

'Whenever I go back, I go to my son's grave without fail.'

She was bending. Bunny could not see her face. He had tea with her. Later on, Mr. Wilson's daughter made a large bouquet of flowers for Bunny. After a while, Sunita came down. She was covered with dust. She wanted a bucket and a mop. She took another hour. The clean bed sheet she had taken out from Simran's cupboard was spread; the curtains, washed and pressed, were hung. The table was covered with a neat, embroidered piece of cloth and small, square cushions were thrown on the sofa. Sunita spread a beige rug, with oblong patterns. The place shone.

'We will order something from outside. I don't expect you to go home and cook.'

Sunita was a reservoir of energy. She dismissed the proposal.

'By the time your mamma comes back from the college, the food would be ready.'

She prepared bread and butter pudding, with vanilla sauce, for dessert.

Praseetha Amma came with her son. Perhaps she was seeing her house for the last time. She roamed around, looking at her house. It was the place where her children had grown. There were old associations. She did not sleep that night. She touched the wall, the door, the window. Life was comfortable with her son, but she yearned to come back and take a last look. Sunita had told Praseetha Amma about William. The old lady wondered what was in Simran's mind.

'I don't know.' Sunita pressed her lips, not able to satisfy the old woman's curiosity. 'William sahib does not come nowadays and memsahib has told me she is not going back to Delhi.'

'I will come to meet Simran tomorrow.'

'I want to thank her for everything.' She added, after a while.

Simran looked at Amma coldly as the old woman probed. Then she smiled.

'Amma, why don't you tell me something about your son and daughter-in-law?'

Amma knew it was difficult to read Simran's mind. And if Simran refused to discuss William, she could do nothing about it.

Amma rose after a while. She peeped into Bunny's room. Bunny got up and touched her feet.

The old lady blessed him.

Bunny left Chennai the following day. It rained lightly. Sunita had accompanied them.

'Ma, Papa misses you.'

'I know.'

She waved as she saw Bunny go.

24

Second Time Free

Simran's loss was colossal. She had lost Varun, the man who had stood by her all these years. They had built their lives block by block; Varun had always been appreciative of his wife's efforts. He had enthused her, encouraged her. Something went wrong somewhere. Varun did not leave Simran; but he was no longer completely hers. Simran hated sharing her man with any other woman.

Simran remembered Swati – an elegent woman, with a will to succeed. She took care of her looks. Men get bored of their wives after a few years, she had read somewhere. They start looking for freshness elsewhere.

She hated Swati from the core of her heart.

At times she felt Swati was a sadder soul. She appeared smart, confident, but there was a sense of loss somewhere.

Simran touched her nose as she remembered Swati, the woman who had given her much pain. She felt no sympathy for her. Simran sat on the rug and stared at her feet. She felt her nails needed a fresh coat of polish. She rose and selected a light shade of pink.

William often said that pink colour suited her.

Simran gave a short laugh. She began painting her nails. Sunita stopped mopping the floor, and looked at her mistress.

Simran had looked for support in William, a man who was younger than her. She tried forgetting Varun, the man who had cheated her, spurned her. Simran's face burnt as she remembered William. The bottle of nail polish fell on the rug. She was not bothered. These things did not bother her any longer.

Simran hated Marilyn in the same way she had disliked Swati. When she thought William was her man, Marilyn re-entered his life. Why was she fated to suffer deprivation every time? When she longed for William, he was with Marilyn. She waited for months, her heart throbbing every time there was a telephone call. She received no call from William. While she yearned for him, he spent his nights with Marilyn.

Simran did not know she could hate any woman so vehemently. Marilyn was the second woman who took away her happiness.

She placed the palms of her hands on the rug, all her fingers outstretched. It took around ten minutes for the nail polish to dry. She smiled, as she remembered William. He loved making presents. That bottle of nail polish was a gift from him.

She remembered Marilyn's face. Her smile disappeared. For the second time, she was sharing her man with another woman.

Sunita brought her a cup of tea. She took small sips. Thoughts clung to her like a child, unwilling to leave the mother. She left the house and started walking, slowly. She looked like a woman in trance. Why does a man you love give you pain? When she looked back, she felt she had had enough.

The end of any relationship is gut wrenching. Many have taken away their lives in desperation.

Simran did not want to die. Simran felt she was a free woman for the second time.

When she returned, Sunita informed her there was call from Bunny. She washed her hands and headed towards her study room. She wanted to send an email to her son.

'I am coming to England,' she pressed the keys feverishly, 'you come to the airport after I send the confirmation.'

She smiled as she switched off the PC.

Simran was leaving Chennai.